Praise for *I'm With Cupid*

"Readers are in for a wild and hilarious ride from upcoming installments in the Switched at First Kiss series."

Booklist

"A cute and mild love stor~ ~harm that dives a little deeper wi~ ~th and love."

~hool Library Journal

"As always, Staniszewski provides a deft mix of comedy and sensitive, deeper themes, making her book not only entertaining, but one that offers wisdom. She knows where to mine the humor from middle school life but does not sacrifice her characterizations for easy laughs. Light—but not lightweight—fun for preteens."

—*Kirkus Reviews*

Praise for *The Dirt Diary*

"Holy fried onion rings! Fun from beginning to end."
—Wendy Mass, *New York Times* bestselling author of
11 Birthdays and *The Candymakers*

"I LOVED it...sweet, sensitive, and delicious!"
—Erin Dionne, author of *Models Don't Eat Chocolate Cookies*

"Confidently addressing a number of common tween troubles that include bullying, parental divorce, and peer pressure, Staniszewski introduces a determined eighth grader desperate to get her separated parents back together in this humorous problem novel."
—*Publishers Weekly*

"Staniszewski neatly captures the pain of a shy young girl with newly separated parents... The quick pace and creative story line will attract those in the mood for an undemanding, light read."
—*Kirkus Reviews*

Praise for *The Prank List*

"*The Prank List* hooks readers with snappy dialogue from the beginning... Rachel is a likable character for middle school readers, who will relate to her problems."

—*VOYA*

"Staniszewski keeps the focus on comedy...but she lets her story become a bit more serious with the pranks Rachel plays. Clearly, Rachel will learn a few life lessons as she stumbles through her summer, but they go down easy in this narrative peppered with such amusing catchphrases as 'Oh my goldfish' and 'What the Shrek?' Gentle fun laced with equally gentle wisdom."

—*Kirkus Reviews*

"Tween readers who find Rachel endearing will find a fast-paced comedy of errors."

—*School Library Journal*

Praise for
My Very UnFairy Tale Life

"Anna Staniszewski creates a magical world that's totally relatable. You'll find yourself wishing you were alongside Jenny fighting against unicorns (who aren't as peaceful as you think) and traveling to fantastical realms."

—GirlsLife.com

"A light comic romp… An eye for imaginative detail mixes with these likable characters and a theme of empathy for others to keep the story appropriate to a younger audience, who easily will identify with Jenny. Charming."

—*Kirkus Reviews*

"Staniszewski's debut is a speedy and amusing ride that displays a confident, on-the-mark brand of humor, mostly through Jenny's wisecracking narration…will keep readers entertained."

—*Publishers Weekly*

Also by Anna Staniszewski

My Very UnFairy Tale Life Series

My Very UnFairy Tale Life

My Epic Fairy Tale Fail

My Sort of Fairy Tale Ending

The Dirt Diary Series

The Dirt Diary

The Prank List

The Gossip File

Switched at First Kiss Series

I'm With Cupid

Finders Reapers

SWITCHED AT
FIRST KISS

ANNA **STANISZEWSKI**

sourcebooks
jabberwocky

Published by Sourcebooks Jabberwocky, an imprint of Sourcebooks, Inc.
P.O. Box 4410, Naperville, Illinois 60567-4410
(630) 961-3900
Fax: (630) 961-2168
www.sourcebooks.com

Library of Congress Cataloging-in-Publication data is on file with the publisher.

Source of Production: Versa Press, East Peoria, Illinois, USA
Date of Production: January 2016
Run Number: 5005603

Printed and bound in the United States of America.
VP 10 9 8 7 6 5 4 3 2 1

For Ray, again.

chapter 1

"C ome on, Lena. Fall!" Lena's best friend Abigail called behind her. Meanwhile, Lena stood with her eyes closed and her arms crossed over her chest mummy-style, trying to will her body to drop backward into Abigail's waiting arms. But she couldn't. Because under Abigail's arms was the hard, wooden, and potentially very painful stage.

"Maybe next time," Lena said finally, opening her eyes.

Abigail groaned. "You're going to have to do a trust fall sometime. Everyone else has already done a bunch."

Lena glanced around the stage. Sure enough, all the other kids in her school's production of *Alice in Wonderland* were flopping around like half-dead fish, throwing themselves into each other's arms. Clearly, Lena's relationship with gravity was a little more complicated than theirs.

She noticed Mr. Jackson giving her a disapproving look from the foot of the stage. He was probably regretting casting her as a playing card. Mr. Jackson was all about "trusting the process and trusting each other." That's why the cast had spent hours over the past few weeks doing team-building exercises and almost zero time on things Lena thought were pretty important, such as making sure that all the cast members actually knew their lines.

She bit back a sigh and swapped places with Abigail.

"You'll catch me, right?" her friend asked. "I really don't want to die before opening night. That would be so embarrassing. Plus, I'd be forced to come back as a ghost and haunt you for the rest of your life."

"Don't worry. You'll be fine," Lena said.

Abigail glanced around the stage. "In fact," she added in a dramatic whisper, "I bet this whole auditorium is filled with ghosts of people who died during trust falls."

Lena had to laugh. She knew for a fact that there weren't any wandering spirits in the entire school, but she couldn't tell her friend that. The only person who knew the truth about Lena's secret identity as a soul collector—besides Lena's boss—was her boyfriend Marcus, and he had a supernatural secret of his own.

As if he could tell she was thinking about him, Marcus came into the auditorium lugging a half-painted wooden tree. Suddenly, Lena found it a lot harder to concentrate on trust falls. She couldn't believe that she and Marcus were going on their official six-week-anniversary date that night.

"Lena, watch out!" Mr. Jackson yelled.

She snapped back to reality in time to see Abigail falling toward her. Lena scrambled to thrust her arms out, barely managing to stop Abigail from hitting the floor.

"Oof!" Abigail said as she landed heavily in Lena's arms.

Mr. Jackson was already marching over, his face redder than his bow tie. "You can't let your partner down like that, Lena! How can you be part of a team when you're not in tune with those around you?"

"I'm sorry! I was…" Lena felt silly finishing that sentence. How could she admit that she'd almost dropped the lead in the play because she'd been distracted thinking about her boyfriend? Lena had dreamed of being onstage since fifth grade. Now that she was finally in the middle school play, was she really going to ruin it by getting moony over a guy? Even if he was a very sweet, supercute one? "I'm sorry," she said again.

Mr. Jackson sighed. "I know you can do better." He turned to the rest of the cast. "Everyone! Remember what I always say?"

"You have to trust the process!" the other kids chanted back at him. Lena forced herself to mouth the words along with them.

"Exactly!" Mr. Jackson grinned and adjusted his red suspenders that perfectly matched his bow tie. Then he clapped his hands and announced that they were done with trust falls.

Lena hoped that meant they'd actually be rehearsing scenes. There were only two weeks to go until opening night after all! But Mr. Jackson informed them that in order to get into their characters' minds, they were going to brainstorm what their characters had eaten for breakfast.

Lena couldn't believe it. Her character was a playing card! What could it possibly eat for breakfast—a bowl of poker chips? But she was sure if she asked Mr. Jackson, he'd be even more disappointed in her. Instead, she glanced out into the auditorium again to find Marcus. But someone else caught her eye.

A girl she'd never seen before was standing in the back row, staring up at the stage. And, unless Lena was imagining things, staring right at her. There was a strange expression on the girl's face, as if she was only half awake.

For a moment, Lena thought she saw an odd haze around the girl's head. It reminded Lena of the auras she'd seen a few weeks ago when she and Marcus had accidentally swapped powers after being dared to kiss at Connie Reynolds's party. Lena had only been a supernatural matchmaker—like Cupid but without the diaper—for a few days, but that had been quite enough time to make her appreciate her soul-collecting job. Maybe the aura meant that this girl was going to be zapped with a love bolt soon.

"Lena?" Abigail asked, touching her shoulder.

"What?" Lena turned to see that the entire cast had cleared off, and she was the only one left standing onstage.

"We're about to run the opening scene."

"Oh, good," Lena said. Finally, they'd get some actual work done at rehearsal.

As she hurried into the wings, she couldn't help glancing back out into the audience to see if the girl was still staring at her. But the back row was empty. Whoever the girl had been, she was gone.

chapter 2

"E ddie sure knows how to pick a date spot," Marcus said, scanning the bowling alley. The place was surprisingly empty for a Friday night, and it reeked of moldy carpet and onion rings. This was definitely not what Marcus had had in mind when he'd planned their big six-week-anniversary date.

"It's not so bad," Lena said, studying the concession stand menu. "Look, you can get two kinds of cheese sauce on your French fries. Double the heart attack!"

Marcus smiled. He'd been planning to bring Lena to a fancy restaurant that his grandfather had once raved about, but then Marcus's boss had called with a last-minute matchmaking assignment and messed it all up.

"We'll have a do-over anniversary date tomorrow, okay?" he asked.

Lena didn't answer. She was focused on something over his shoulder. "Look, it's Hayleigh and Abigail. What are they doing here?"

He followed her gaze and spotted Lena's two best friends in one of the lanes, along with a few kids from the school play. "Um, bowling?" he asked.

Lena was already heading over to them, so Marcus hurried to catch up.

"Hey," Abigail said, pushing her pale ponytail over her shoulder. "Some of us were running lines after rehearsal, but we got bored and came here instead." She lowered her voice. "Of course, I had to call Hayleigh since you-know-who is here."

They all looked at Emery Higgins, who was playing the Cheshire Cat in the play. He was focused on picking something out of his braces while Hayleigh was making a big show of begging him to blow on her bowling ball for luck. It was a well-known fact that Hayleigh had a serious crush on Emery. A well-known fact to everyone except him.

"We're about to start a new game if you want to play with us," Abigail offered.

That sounded fun, but Marcus's phone buzzed, reminding him why he was here. "Maybe later. Um, I have to go do… the thing."

"Oh right," Lena said. "How about I bowl for you until you get back?" She waved him away with a little wink.

He flashed her a grateful smile as he hurried away. It was awesome how he and Lena were always on the same wavelength. To think, only a couple months ago, they'd barely even been friends!

When he was on the other side of the shoe rental counter, he stopped and scanned the bowling alley for Peter Chung, age fifteen. After a minute of searching, he still hadn't spotted the telltale gray aura that usually meant a person needed a love boost.

Maybe Peter was in the bathroom. It wasn't Marcus's favorite spot to zap people, but being a matchmaker wasn't always the most glamorous job. Just the week before, he'd had to match a couple right next to a Dumpster outside a seafood restaurant. Nothing went with true love like the smell of rotting fish.

He heard Lena's laugh echoing nearby and turned to see her and Abigail looking at him and whispering. Clearly, they were talking about him. Lena's face was glowing with happiness, as if the mere sight of Marcus made her smile. He knew exactly how she felt.

Focus, Marcus told himself.

Finally, he spotted a teenage guy coming in through the front door of the bowling alley. There was a faint gray haze around his head that only Marcus could see, and he could even *feel* the loneliness wafting from him.

"Peter, there you are!" Marcus called out before realizing he'd actually spoken the words aloud.

Peter frowned at him. "Do I know you?"

"Oh, um, no," Marcus said as his phone started to beep in his pocket. It was time. "But you know my sister, Ann-Marie Torelli?" He had no idea if Peter actually knew his sister, but they did both go to the same high school.

Peter's face lit up. "She's, like, the best runner in the district."

"I'm Marcus." As he held out his hand, Marcus heard Lena's tinkling laugh ringing across the bowling alley. He ignored the sound and willed his energy to spark. Instantly, his fingers flared to life with a red glow that seemed brighter than usual. Maybe that meant this match would be his best one yet.

Focus, he told himself again. Then he grabbed Peter's hand and shook it.

The energy left Marcus's fingers and shot into Peter's so fast that Marcus stumbled back. When the energy was gone, relief washed over him. The first moments after an assignment were always exhausting and satisfying at the same time.

Meanwhile, a dazed look swept over Peter's face as if he'd been bopped in the head with a frying pan. Then he turned and smiled blearily at a tall, skinny girl who was walking toward him. Her face was streaked with so much makeup that she kind of looked like an Easter egg. She was definitely not Marcus's type, but if she and Peter were a match, that was all that mattered.

"Hey, I'm Peter!" he called out to the girl.

Her entire face lit up. "I'm Claire!"

Marcus watched with satisfaction as a yellow aura bloomed around the couple and sparks started to swirl between them, little bits of light that only he could see.

Then something changed. The yellow aura grew even brighter, almost neon, and one by one, the sparks flared until they were nearly blinding. They started bouncing around so furiously, Marcus thought they might shoot through the ceiling.

He expected Peter and Claire to break eye contact after a minute and start chatting and laughing like he'd seen all his other matches do, but they simply stood there and dreamily peered into each other's eyes. Their gazes were so intense, it was almost scary. He wasn't sure Claire was even breathing.

"Um, guys?" Marcus finally said. Nothing. He took a hesitant step forward and snapped his fingers in front of their faces. Finally, they both blinked and took a step away from each other.

"Can I buy you some fries?" Peter asked, holding out his hand.

Claire nodded eagerly and thrust her hand in his. "And a milk shake!" They skipped—actually skipped!—away, a shower of sparks shooting around them like fireworks. As they turned toward the concession stand, Peter leaped into the air and joyfully clicked his heels together like a cartoon character.

Marcus stared after them in disbelief. He'd done almost a dozen matches, and none had ever gone like this. Uh-oh. Were his powers still messed up after he and Lena had swapped abilities a few weeks ago? Eddie had said everything was back to normal, but what if he was wrong?

Marcus made himself take a deep breath. He was being paranoid. The four matches he'd done since the whole power-swapping fiasco had all gone fine. Besides, even though the connection between Peter and Claire seemed unusually intense, the two were clearly happy. That was all that mattered. His boss had told him that his powers would eventually grow stronger. Maybe it had come sooner than expected, that's all.

"Are you okay?" Lena asked, coming up beside him.

"Yeah, I'm great." No need to share his paranoia with her. Still, he couldn't help asking: "Do your soul-collecting assignments ever go a little *too* well?"

She frowned. "What do you mean?"

"Like, your energy shoots out and the soul gets sent to the After faster than it should? Maybe things seem more intense than normal?"

Lena shook her head and glanced around as if to make sure no one was listening. "But soul collecting is different," she said softly. "There's not much wiggle room with life and death. Love is…less strict."

"Love has just as many rules as death does," Marcus said. Lena had finally warmed up to the idea that love wasn't merely chemicals tricking you into feeling things, but she still wasn't comfortable with the whole idea of love matches and soul mates.

"Oh boy," Lena said, rolling her eyes. "We're definitely not having this argument again!" She laughed. "Come on. It's your turn to bowl. I put the perfect bowling name for you up on the scoreboard."

"Spare Diaper?" Marcus guessed.

Lena grinned. "Lovestruck."

He grinned back, taking her hand in his. "Perfect."

chapter 3

C hipmunk, you're just in time!" Lena's dad called when she got home from her date. For once, he wasn't watching some boring TV show about the history of clocks. Instead, her dad was typing away on his laptop with the local news on in the background. "I'm filling out my online dating profile. Do you want to help?"

"You're doing *what*?" Lena asked as Professor ran up to her with a mysterious piece of old flannel in his mouth. He wagged his German shepherd tail a few times and then dropped the fabric at her feet before trotting back to the sliding glass door. These days, Professor spent most of his time watching his squirrel wife (one of the unfortunate side effects of Lena and Marcus's power-swapping fiasco) scampering around the yard. It had gotten too cold for him to be out in the nest they'd built together.

Her dad laughed lightly. "I told my sister I was thinking of getting back into the dating scene, and she suggested I try Internet dating."

"Does this mean Aunt Teresa is done trying to fix you up with people?"

"She blames herself for things not working out with Marguerite, so she's encouraging me to try new dating avenues."

Sadly, that whole disaster had actually been Lena's fault. She'd pushed too hard to make her dad and Marguerite's relationship work, even using Marcus's matchmaking powers when she knew it was a bad idea. She thought she'd been helping her dad, but she'd only been prolonging the agony.

As Lena went into the kitchen to grab a glass of water, she could hear a news story on TV about a hospital in a nearby town that had recently been named "The Most Haunted Spot in the Country."

"Why are they reporting on ghost stories?" she heard her dad mutter at the TV. "The news should be for real facts!"

Lena smiled to herself. If only her dad knew the truth about her secret identity, he might reconsider what "real facts" were. But even if she could tell her brain scientist dad about being a soul collector, Lena wasn't sure he'd believe her, not even if he could do a hundred scans and studies to prove it. Besides, Lena had no desire to have her dad poking around in her brain.

"You can always change the channel," Lena started to say. But she stopped cold when she saw the kitchen table. Every inch of it was covered in pieces of white foam that had been cut into tiny diamonds.

"Um, Dad?" she called, poking her head back into the living room. "Is that supposed to be my costume?"

His face lit up. "Yes, indeed! It's not finished yet, of course. But when I'm done measuring and cutting the pieces, it'll take no time to assemble them."

"But the instructions said to use a big piece of foam and cut out armholes and stuff. That's what Justin Alvarez is doing for his playing card costume."

Her father shook his head. "I came up with a much better way. You'll see. Your costume will be far more aerodynamic than his."

"In case I need to make a quick getaway off the stage?" Lena asked.

"Exactly," he said, not picking up on her sarcastic tone. She loved her dad, but for a super smart person, he could be pretty clueless.

"You know, Dad, I can make my own costume. It's not a big deal."

His dark eyebrows drooped. "But all the other parents are making them."

He said "parents" but what he meant was "moms." Lena was the only one in the play whose mom wasn't around to do things like that. She knew her dad felt bad about that fact, and that's why he'd volunteered for costume duty, even though he was a million times more comfortable with an MRI machine than a sewing one.

"Okay," Lena said softly. "I'm sure your way is fine." She did appreciate her dad trying to help, but maybe it wouldn't be a bad idea to make herself a backup costume just in case.

She turned to go to her room, but her dad called, "Hold on, Chipmunk! Would you say I'm 'ruggedly handsome' or 'boyishly good-looking'?"

Lena choked down a laugh. Something like "sweetly nerdy" was more fitting, but she couldn't exactly tell him that. "How about both?"

"Good idea! By the way, how about you bring this boyfriend of yours over for dinner this week?" He said it as a question, but Lena could tell her dad had already made up his mind. "I promise I won't try to cook. We'll order pizza."

"Oh, um…" She wanted her dad to meet Marcus and vice versa, but it also felt like a big step. Then again, maybe it was better to get the big meet and greet over with. At least she was pretty confident that they'd get along. "Okay, I'll invite him."

As Lena retreated to her room, her thoughts went back to the play. It seemed like she was the only person in the whole cast who was worried about the show. But how could Lena relax when the Cheshire Cat kept forgetting his lines and none of the other playing cards knew when to make their entrances? (During the last run-through, Justin Alvarez had actually come on three scenes early!) She knew Mr. Jackson would only tell her to "trust the process" again, so Lena supposed she'd have to try harder, even though they were running out of time. Opening night was supposed to be sooner, in fact, but a pipe had burst in the auditorium over Thanksgiving, and the show had been pushed back. Lena hoped that hadn't been a bad omen. Not that she believed in those sorts of things.

She sighed and examined the quilt she'd been working on. As she started sorting through squares of fabric, she felt her mood lifting. Quilting usually had that effect on her. It was hard to be irrational when your hands were working on something so orderly.

The quilt was going to be her mom's Christmas present this year. The holidays were still a few weeks away, but this was Lena's most ambitious project yet, so she wanted to give herself plenty of time to finish it. Christmas was the one time of year that Lena saw her mom ever since she'd left back when Lena was in fifth grade. She couldn't wait to show her mom how much she'd learned on her own, without her help.

Just when she was making some real progress laying out the pattern, Lena's phone rang. It was her boss Eduardo, a.k.a.

Eddie. Funnily enough, he was also Marcus's matchmaking boss. Apparently there was a supernatural staffing shortage or something. But why was he calling her so late?

"I wanted to tell you that you have a collection coming up tomorrow morning," he said in his faint Spanish accent.

"Since when do you give me so much notice?" Not that Lena was complaining. She often wished her boss would give her more than the usual half hour warning—an hour if she was lucky.

"It will also be a training session," he said. "I'm sending a new soul collector with you. Her name is Natalie, and she's new to the area. She'll meet you at your house in the morning."

"I've only been doing this for a few months. Are you sure I'm the right person for the job?"

There was a long pause, and Lena could hear her boss shooting zombies in the background. It was pretty ironic that the guy who was supposed to help Lena guide souls into the afterlife loved playing games where he had to fight entire armies of the undead. The only time Eddie wasn't destroying zombies during one of their conversations was when he was testing out his newest tech gadgets—then she'd usually hear faint beeping instead of gunfire. Eddie had to be around Lena's dad's age, but sometimes he acted a lot more like the guys at Lena's school.

"You were fantastic with Marcus when you had to teach

him how to use your powers," he said. "I'm sure you'll be a natural, kid."

Lena couldn't help sitting up a little straighter. No one was immune to flattery after all. Her dad had even done a study on it once. "I'll give it a shot. What's the assignment?"

"I've already sent it to your phone," Eddie said. She expected him to hang up so he could hurry back to his game, but he cleared his throat and added, "I've been meaning to ask how things are going with you and Marcus."

Ew. Was her boss really asking about personal stuff like that? Still, she smiled as she said, "Good. It's our one-and-a-half-month anniversary this weekend." It seemed a little silly to celebrate the day that they'd kissed at her audition and swapped their powers back, but Marcus was so excited about it that she couldn't help getting swept up in it too.

"Nothing unusual has happened recently?"

"I thought everything went back to normal after my audition. Didn't it?"

"Of course. I only wanted to make sure it was all still going well." Another chorus of zombie screams erupted on the other end of the line. "Gotta go. Have fun tomorrow!" Eddie added, as if anyone could have a good time collecting souls. But before she could point that out, he'd already hung up.

chapter 4

Marcus spent Saturday morning slogging through a copy of *Quilting for Beginners* that Lena had lent him. He carefully leafed through, feeling like he should be wearing white gloves to keep from smudging the pristine pages. If it wasn't for the "From the Library of Lena Perris" sticker pasted neatly in the front, Marcus would have thought the book had never even been opened.

The longer he stared at the book, the more his eyelids drooped. Marcus glanced longingly at the model space station waiting on his worktable and finally put the book down. So much for impressing Lena that night with his knowledge of interfacing and batting—whatever those were.

As he got to his feet, a faint "meow" echoed through his room. It was coming from the little ball of light curled up next to his pillow. As crazy as it sounded, Marcus had wound up with a pet ghost cat after he'd accidentally used Lena's soul-collecting powers on it. He kept waiting for the cat's soul to disappear, the way Eddie said it would, but so far it seemed happy to hang around Marcus's house, even though he was the only one who could see it.

Marcus settled at his worktable in front of the space station that he'd recently found at a yard sale. Once he repaired and painted it, it would be good as new. He'd already started asking around at school to see if anyone would want to buy it. It would be hard to let the model go after all that work, but if he was going to get Lena the perfect Christmas present—tickets to see *A Midsummer Night's Dream*, her favorite play—he would need every dollar he could scrape together. He was planning to use the allowance money he'd been saving up for his and Lena's do-over six-week-anniversary date that night.

After a second, he glanced at the robot model displayed above his table. It was his favorite, not because it was the most impressive, but because it was the first one he'd ever worked on by himself. Grandpa Joe had guided him through it, but he'd let Marcus do all the work on his own. He sighed, suddenly missing his grandfather so much that it felt like his insides might cave in.

Loud footsteps erupted in the hallway, and Marcus managed to pull himself together before his sister threw open his bedroom door.

"Why don't you ever knock?" he demanded. Out of the corner of his eye, he saw the ghost cat scamper off the bed and jump onto his bookcase. In true cat fashion, it knocked a magazine onto the floor with its invisible tail before disappearing into Marcus's closet.

"Whoa. What was that?" Ann-Marie asked, staring at the magazine. To her, it must have looked like it had flown off the shelf by itself.

"The wind," Marcus said, biting back a smile.

His sister scowled at the locked window and then, without asking, plopped down on Marcus's bed.

"Did you want something?" he asked.

Ann-Marie's perpetual scowl deepened. "Why did you tell a guy at the bowling alley that you know me?"

Marcus looked at her. "How did you find out about that?"

"One of the girls from the track team was there with Peter Chung, and she texted me when he told her what you'd said. Why were you talking to him about me?"

There was no way to explain things to Ann-Marie without revealing his secret. And even if Marcus could tell her the truth about his matchmaking powers, she'd probably tell him to stop drinking so much soda, since it was obviously rotting his teeth *and* his brain.

"I-I thought he looked familiar," Marcus stammered. "Like s-someone I'd seen you hanging around with."

His sister let out a cheerless laugh. "I'm surprised he even knows who I am. Unless he knows I'm the coach's daughter or something. He does go to all the hockey games."

"He didn't mention Dad or hockey, but he did say you were the best runner in the district."

His sister's eyebrows went up. "Really?" Something like a smile crept over her face for a second, but then the scowl returned. "Well, he has a new girlfriend now, so it doesn't matter."

"Ann-Marie!" Their dad's voice rang out in the hall. "Time to head to the track!" A second later, their dad appeared in Marcus's doorway with a sports drink in his hand. "What are you two doing in here?"

"Nothing," Ann-Marie said, getting to her feet. Marcus expected her to rush out the door like she always did when it was time to go train. But she hesitated, almost like she wanted to keep talking to him. That had definitely never happened before.

"Marcus, what's this about you being in the school play?" his dad asked, wrinkling his nose. "I hope you're not doing it for Lena. No point wasting your time mooning over a girl when you should be doing your homework."

Ah, yes. His dad, the hopeless romantic. Sometimes Marcus wondered how his parents had ever gotten together. They must have been zapped by a seriously powerful matchmaker.

"I'm doing sets for the play because it's fun," Marcus said.

In fact, painting fake trees and dragging them around was the opposite of fun, but he wasn't about to admit that his dad was right and that he was only doing it to spend more time with Lena.

"We're leaving in three minutes," his dad said to Ann-Marie. Then he strode out of the room.

Ann-Marie turned to leave too, but then she hovered in the doorway for a second. "Anyway, stop telling people we're related, okay? Especially guys like Peter."

"Fine, sorry," Marcus said.

As Ann-Marie left the room, Marcus caught a hint of a grayish aura around her head. Then a wave of sadness hit him like a slap. He sucked in a breath. The feeling was so overwhelming, it made him dizzy.

Only when his sister closed the door behind her did the sensation fade.

Whoa. Was it possible that Ann-Marie had a crush on Peter Chung? It was hard to believe she had time to notice guys when her whole life was about running and school, but there was no other way to explain the sadness radiating from her.

Suddenly, he felt terrible. His sister had never been the bubbly type, but he'd had no idea she was so lonely. And now, thanks to his latest match, she was more miserable than ever.

chapter 5

Lena was stunned to find the girl she'd seen in the auditorium the previous day waiting for her at the end of her driveway in the morning. This was Natalie, the new soul collector Eddie wanted her to train? Suddenly, the strange aura Lena had seen made a little more sense. She must have sensed that this girl was supernatural like she was.

Natalie waved enthusiastically from the mailbox. She was pretty, with honey-colored hair and delicate features. Lena's dad had once told her that people whose faces were symmetrical were considered the most attractive, which made Lena curious to measure Natalie's face with a ruler. She was willing to bet both sides were pretty much identical.

"You must be Natalie," Lena said, studying the girl carefully. She'd never met another soul collector before, but there was nothing about Natalie that screamed "death." Then again, Lena hoped there wasn't anything about *her* that made people instantly think of crypts and coffins. Being a soul collector probably sounded pretty grim to the average person, but Lena wasn't killing anyone or anything, only guiding people's souls to the After. She was like a paranormal usher.

"I'm so excited you're here!" Natalie chirped. "I can't wait to talk to someone about all this! It's hard enough being new in town without having a brand-new, huge secret on top of it."

Lena knew all about keeping secrets. It had been a relief to be able to tell Marcus about the part of her life that she had to keep hidden from everyone else. She couldn't blame Natalie for wanting that too.

"I think I saw you at school yesterday," Lena said. "During play rehearsal."

The girl gave her a blank look. "You did?"

"You were in the back of the auditorium watching us doing theater games. You probably thought we were all nuts. After you left, the director actually had us sneeze as our characters."

Natalie chuckled. "Oh, I remember now! I was walking around the school, checking it out! I must have peeked into the auditorium!" Natalie's voice was so light and cheerful that it sounded like every sentence out of her mouth ended in an exclamation point. "Should we get started?" she added.

"Follow me." Lena waved her down the driveway. "So where do you live?" she asked as they turned onto the sidewalk.

"On Maple Street, right near the Y!"

"My boyfriend Marcus lives in your neighborhood," Lena said. "He's a matchmaker, which basically means he zaps people with love spells."

"How fun! I had a boyfriend back home, but we broke up when I found out I was moving. He wasn't supernatural or anything though!" Natalie laughed. "Wow, I love your bag!"

Lena held up her quilted messenger bag, one of her latest creations. "I made it a couple weeks ago. If you want, I can show you how sometime."

"That would be great! Thanks!"

Lena couldn't help grinning back at her. She couldn't remember the last time she'd felt so instantly comfortable around someone. Maybe it was because Natalie was so friendly, or maybe everything Lena had gone through with Marcus and the power swap had helped open her up to people in more ways than she'd realized.

When they got to the address that Eddie had sent to her phone, Lena hopped up the steps and tried the doorknob. As she expected, the front door swung open.

"Doors are usually unlocked," Lena whispered. "And people don't really notice us, but I still try to be quiet. Are you ready?"

Natalie nodded and followed Lena inside. The house was small and cluttered, the walls covered in faded family photographs and dusty paintings of seascapes. They crept into the living room, where an old woman was sitting on the couch watching the news. She was stooped and thin, with an oxygen tank parked beside her on the carpet. It was clear she'd been sick for a long time.

"Can you see her soul?" Lena whispered. "It's like a little light in the person's chest." According to her manual, soul collectors could see souls even when they weren't assigned to them. Ever since she and Marcus had swapped powers, Lena had also been able to see a hint of the matchmaking auras, but she was pretty sure that was rare, since her manual didn't say anything about it.

Natalie squinted at the old woman's torso for a minute and then shook her head. "I'm not sure!" Even when she was whispering, her voice was full of excitement.

"Your powers are still new, so you might not sense souls right away," Lena said. "Plus this one's pretty faint. That means she doesn't have much time left." As if on cue, a soft alarm went off on Lena's phone. "Now I focus on the soul and on calling up my energy and then—"

She waited for her fingers to flare a deep purple, but for a second, nothing happened. Lena blinked in surprise and tried again. This time, her fingers instantly began to glow. She flashed Natalie an embarrassed smile. Clearly, having an audience was making it hard for Lena to focus.

"When my fingers start glowing, that means I'm ready to send the soul to the After," Lena explained.

She took a couple steps toward the couch until she was directly beside the old woman. Then she placed her glowing hand on the woman's frail shoulder. The energy rushed out of her fingertips and disappeared. Lena stumbled back, a little light-headed.

"Are you okay?" Natalie asked, her eyes wide.

Lena steadied herself on the back of an armchair. "It's normal to be dizzy for a second. But you're also relieved because you can feel the soul detaching from its body and being set free."

Natalie's gaze swung back to the old woman. "And now she's going to die?"

"It'll happen in the next couple of minutes, but we can leave before it does."

Natalie didn't move. "Are they usually alone like this at the end?" She didn't seem sad or afraid like Lena would have expected, only curious.

"Most have family and friends with them. But even if they don't, their souls are happy after they move on. Come on," Lena said, gently pulling Natalie away. "Let's give her some privacy."

As they slipped out of the house, Lena's phone buzzed. It was a message from Marcus: My sister has a crush on the guy I zapped last night!

Lena wrote back, Oops! She had to smile at the thought of Marcus's sourpuss sister having a crush on anyone. Then again, if Marcus could have a ghost cat living in his house, Lena supposed anything was possible.

They headed back down the street, Natalie suddenly quiet. Maybe the assignment had gotten to her after all.

"That woman's energy is moving from one place to another," Lena told her. "It's not so bad if you think about it that way." In fact, the idea made Lena feel safe somehow. If energy never disappeared, that meant even if you lost someone, that person wasn't really gone.

Natalie shrugged. "Actually, I was thinking that it's not as bad as I was expecting. You're helping people, right?"

"Exactly. Without us, their souls would wander around, lost and confused. Then soul hunters would have to track them down, and the cosmic balance could get all messed up." Eddie loved going on about "the order of the universe." At first, Lena had thought he was being dramatic, but after her and Marcus's powers had started going haywire after their first kiss and affecting other people's assignments, she'd realized how important keeping the universe happy was.

"Eddie was right about you being a natural at soul collecting," Natalie said, sounding impressed.

"I guess it's thanks to my mom," Lena answered. She

was surprised at herself for mentioning her mother to a total stranger, but Natalie was easy to talk to. "She was a nurse for really sick people, so she didn't sugarcoat anything. That's why I'm not freaked out by the idea of people dying. Did Eddie tell you why you were chosen for the job?"

Natalie didn't answer. She'd suddenly gone very still, her eyes focused on a far-off spot.

"Natalie?" Lena asked. But the girl only stood there like a statue. Not even her hair moved in the breeze. "Are you okay?"

An instant later, Natalie blinked. "What? Oh, yeah. Sorry! I kind of spaced out for a second." She grabbed a small green notebook from her pocket and started furiously scribbling in it.

Lena waited awkwardly for her to finish. She was curious to know what Natalie was writing so frantically and what that weird episode had been, but she figured it would be rude to ask.

Finally, when Natalie's pen stopped moving, Lena said, "Is everything okay?"

"Yup! It's great!" Natalie said, tucking the notebook into her pocket as if the whole incident hadn't happened.

Lena wanted to press, but she couldn't blame Natalie for not wanting to share her secrets when they'd only known each other for an hour. "Are you going to be in school on Monday?" Lena asked instead. "I can wait for you out front and show you around."

Natalie's face lit up. "Sure! I really appreciate how nice you're being to me."

As Lena watched Natalie hurry away, she couldn't help smiling to herself. Not only did she have an awesome boyfriend and a part in the play, but now she had a friend she could talk to about her powers, someone who understood. She couldn't believe how well everything was falling into place.

chapter 6

Marcus hadn't meant to arrive at Lena's house early, but he'd been so excited about redoing their anniversary date that he'd headed over as soon as he was ready. He parked his bike at the end of Lena's driveway and then hovered near her recycling bin with a bouquet in his hands, waiting for it to be exactly six o'clock before he rang the doorbell.

According to the book Grandpa Joe had given him, a dating guide from the 1950s, you should always be prompt but not early. Marcus wasn't sure the book's advice had actually gotten Lena to notice him, but he was convinced it had brought him luck. Now that his grandfather was gone, Marcus had been keeping the book with him more and more. Every time he read it, he could almost hear Grandpa's voice. He only hoped his relationship with Lena could be half as perfect as Grandpa Joe and Grandma Lily's had been.

At 5:55, Lena's front door swung open. "What are you doing out there?" she called down the driveway. "Come in!"

Marcus flashed a sheepish grin as he hurried up to meet her. "Sorry I'm early." His freshly ironed clothes were stiff on his body, and he couldn't get used to the helmet-like feeling of gel in his hair, but he'd wanted to look nice for Lena.

"It's okay," she said, waving him inside. "You smell nice."

"Thanks!" The dating book had suggested wearing cologne on a date, so Marcus had swiped some of his dad's, even though the strong scent made his eyes itch. Clearly, the book had been right.

"I was ready a half hour ago, so I've been working on my part," Lena went on. "I know I only have one line in the whole play, but it can't hurt to practice, right?"

He smiled and held out the bouquet of exotic-looking flowers. "These are for you." He hadn't thought to bring flowers the day before, but luckily he was getting a second chance to make this night perfect.

"Thank you!" she said, giving him a peck on the cheek. She headed into the kitchen to put the bouquet in some water.

After she'd displayed the flowers on the table, Marcus caught her giving him a strange look. "What?" he asked.

"Your hair." She brushed at a strand near his forehead, as if trying to dislodge some of the gel. "I think I like it better when it curls around your ears. It's cute." She gave him an adorable smile and shrugged. "So, where are we going?"

"Well, I was thinking we—"

Before he could finish, Lena sneezed. And then again, and again, a rapid burst of sneezes that were so loud, they sounded like gunfire. She backed away from the vase, her eyes suddenly red and watering.

"Are you okay?" Marcus asked.

"I think I might be…" *Achoo!* "Allergic to the flowers." *Achoo!*

"Oh no! I'm sorry!" Marcus tried to grab the bouquet off the table, but he only managed to knock the vase onto the floor, splattering water and petals everywhere.

He gasped and started to clean it up as Lena rushed off to the bathroom, where he could hear her sneezing up a storm. What was wrong with him? Couldn't he even get the whole "giving a girl flowers" thing right?

"Thanks, boy," Marcus said as Professor lapped up most of the water from the floor.

After the last of the offending blooms were in the garbage, Lena came out of the bathroom, dabbing at her nose with a tissue.

"Are you sure you're okay?" Marcus asked.

"I'm fine!" She chuckled. "It's weird though. I've never had an allergic reaction before. I think you must have found the only flowers on earth that I'm allergic to."

Of course he had. "Well, if you're sure. I was thinking we

could go out to dinner." He told her about the fancy French restaurant where he remembered Grandpa Joe had brought Grandma Lily for a wedding anniversary years ago. "Is that okay?"

Lena nodded and gently took his hand in hers. "Anywhere is fine, as long as I'm there with you."

When they went into the restaurant, Lena was suddenly self-conscious about her outfit. "Why didn't you warn me this place was so fancy?" she asked Marcus, glancing at the candlelit tables and the sparkling chandeliers. "I feel so grubby."

"You look perfect," he said, and the sincerity in his voice made her relax.

They walked by a sleek TV built into the wall that was showing the news about some crazy woman who'd dangled over the side of a skyscraper using a rope so she could paint "I love you, Bob" for the whole world to see.

"Wow," Lena said, pointing at the TV. "You'd think a greeting card would be enough."

"Don't you think a big, romantic gesture is nice sometimes?" Marcus asked. "It tells the person that you really do care."

"I guess," Lena said doubtfully. Back when she'd still been convinced that "people in love" were merely ruled by the chemicals in their brains, she would have rolled her eyes at their over-the-top romantic gestures. Now that she and Marcus were together, she could sort of understand them, but she was still pretty sure she'd never risk her life to tell him how much he meant to her.

When they sat down at a table and started studying the menu, it took Lena a minute to realize that it wasn't in another language but simply filled with foods she'd never heard of. She glanced up and saw Marcus's forehead scrunched in concentration.

"So what's good here?" she asked.

He looked up from his menu, his cheeks turning pink. "I have no idea," he admitted. "Grandpa said this place was one of my grandmother's favorites, but I don't know if any of this stuff is even edible. What's Gruyère? It sounds like some kind of fungus."

"I think it might be a type of cheese," Lena said. "We could ask the waiter."

After a few more minutes of confusion, they gave up and waved him over. The waiter reluctantly helped them pick out a few items on the menu, clearly unhappy about serving a couple of ignorant kids.

While they waited for their food, Lena told Marcus about Natalie.

"She doesn't wear a grim reaper outfit, does she?" Marcus asked. "They probably won't let her bring a scythe to school. How would she fit it in her locker?"

Lena kicked him under the table. "She's nice. And I can't believe I'll actually have another soul collector to talk to!"

Marcus nodded. "I hope I get to meet a matchmaker one day. I know Eddie used to be one, but I don't think that counts."

"You think he'll ever tell us what he did to get on probation?" Lena asked. She'd tried to ask Eddie about it a couple of times, but he'd only brushed it off.

"Maybe he played too many video games and kept missing his assignments," Marcus said.

Lena chuckled. "Or he tried to use some weird matchmaking gadget and wound up electrocuting people instead."

When the food came, Lena didn't think it was that bad, but Marcus only picked at his. "It kind of reminds me of slime," he whispered. "Sorry. I thought this place would be better."

Lena touched his hand across the table. "It's fine, Marcus. It's just a random anniversary anyway, isn't it? Most people don't do six weeks."

"I know, but most people also don't swap powers. Besides, six weeks ago, we not only switched our powers back, but we also finally admitted how we felt about each other. I'd say that's plenty to celebrate."

"That's true," she said. "If all of that hadn't happened, I'd probably still have a crush on you and not realize it." She couldn't help sighing as she stabbed a piece of wilted lettuce. "And I wouldn't be in the play."

Marcus frowned. "I thought you were dying to be in *Alice*."

"It's just…I thought it would be different."

"Things looked pretty good at the last rehearsal." Marcus shook his head in wonder. "I still can't believe you talked me into helping with the sets. Remember what happened the last time I set foot on a stage?"

Lena couldn't help laughing. "That was in kindergarten!"

"Still," he said with a shudder, "maybe I *should* start wearing a diaper, just in case. We don't want history repeating itself. Besides, then I'd be more like a real cupid."

"I'm serious, Marcus. What if the show is bad?" Yes, she only had a tiny part, but she still wanted her first play to go perfectly.

"It'll be fine," Marcus assured her as the waiter came to drop off the bill. Before she could even think of offering to pay, Marcus slid some money across the table. "My treat."

"But—"

"It was my idea to come here," he said. "And plus, I want to."

Lena was tempted to argue—this restaurant wasn't cheap!—but she could tell by the look on his face that he wasn't going to back down. "Okay, thank you," she said finally. "But next time, the slime is on me, okay?"

He smiled. "Deal."

chapter 7

"Aren't you freezing?" Lena couldn't help asking when she spotted Natalie on the front steps of the school on Monday morning. The other girl wasn't wearing a jacket, even though it was so cold out that Lena's toes felt numb in her thick socks.

Natalie waved a dismissive hand. "Where I used to live was way colder than this."

"Where was that?" Lena asked, but Natalie was already rushing up the stairs.

"Come on! Let's go find your friends!" she called, her light hair blowing after her. She looked so relaxed and carefree, as if going into a new school wasn't a big deal. Lena wished she could be half that laid-back about things.

She led Natalie down the eighth-grade hallway, deafening with the sounds of kids laughing and chatting.

"So have you gone on any more collecting assignments?" Lena asked softly. When Eddie had sent Lena on her first one, he'd made sure to follow up with another one a couple days later so that she could get used to her new job.

"Oh, no. Not yet," Natalie said. "Soon though, I'm sure!"

When they got to the end of the hall, Lena's excitement at introducing Natalie to her friends dimmed when she saw Hayleigh tearfully shoving books into her locker. Beside her, Abigail was cooing sympathetically, clearly trying to cheer Hayleigh up.

"What's wrong?" Lena asked.

"Hayleigh heard a rumor that Emery likes someone in the play," Abigail explained.

"Do you think it's Fiona?" Hayleigh asked with a hiccup. "She *is* good as the Red Queen. Or that mousy girl, what's her name, the one who never brushes her hair? Why would he like her over me? *Why?*"

"Whoa, calm down," Lena said, afraid her friend might hyperventilate. "How do you know it's not you? You're doing costumes for the play. Doesn't that count?"

"That's what I've been trying to tell her!" Abigail said, throwing her hands up in frustration.

Hayleigh's dark forehead crinkled. "Maybe you're both right," she said, but she didn't sound convinced. She wiped her eyes and finally seemed to notice the unfamiliar girl standing next to Lena. "Oh, who's this?"

"Oops, sorry," Lena said. "Guys, this is Natalie. Today's her first day."

"Nice to meet you!" Natalie said brightly, as if she met crying girls all the time.

Hayleigh gave Natalie a weak wave. "Sorry, I'm not usually such a mess."

"It's okay," Natalie said. "But I don't think you should worry so much about that Emery guy. You're not really his type." She flashed a smile and added, "I should go get my schedule. Lena, find me at lunch, okay?" Then she headed toward the main office.

"If she's new, how does she know Emery?" Abigail asked.

Lena watched Natalie turn the corner. "Maybe she was trying to be encouraging."

Hayleigh dabbed at her eyes with the edge of her sleeve. "It was still kind of a weird thing to say. How do you know her?"

"My boss introduced us," Lena said, still distracted.

"Your boss?" Hayleigh repeated, adjusting her sparkly headband. She had an unwritten rule that she had to wear at least one glittery fashion item per day. "I didn't know you had a job."

Lena blinked. "I meant my dad's boss. He and Natalie's family kind of know each other, so he thought...you know." She hated lying to her friends, especially when she was so terrible at coming up with excuses.

As they headed off to their homerooms, Lena spotted Marcus at the end of the hall. She went to call out his name but paused when she realized he was with Caspar Brown, the biggest bully in school. Why were they talking in the middle of the hallway like they were friends? Last she'd heard, Caspar was still steering clear of Marcus after the ghost cat had attacked him.

Suddenly, she saw Marcus give Caspar something covered in bubble wrap and Caspar slip some cash into Marcus's hand. Then Caspar hurried down the hallway as Marcus went over to his locker, shoving the money into his bag.

What on earth?

"I'll see you guys later," she told her friends.

When Marcus saw her approaching, his face brightened. "Hey, Lena! I had a great idea!"

"What's going on?"

She expected him to explain what the exchange with Caspar had been about, but instead he said, "You know how I told you my sister has a crush on Peter Chung? Well, I decided I'm going to fix her up with someone else so she'll get over him. And what better place to do that than at her track meet tonight? Do you want to come with me?"

"Wait," she said, momentarily forgetting about Caspar. "What if you only make her miserable like I did with my dad and Marguerite? Or what if your powers backfire?" She glanced at Brent Adamson leaning against his locker, the guy she'd foolishly tried to zap with a love boost. The spell had only made him violently ill at the sight of her. Even now, weeks later, he still got a little pale whenever he looked in her direction.

"I was thinking of fixing her up the old-fashioned way. No zap required." Marcus held up the dating book his grandpa had given him, protected by a quilted cover that Lena had made. "So do you want to come?"

"Sorry, I can't. We're actually rehearsing my scene today." Lena waited for Marcus to say something about Caspar, but he didn't. Was he purposely keeping it a secret?

"What?" he asked, self-consciously smoothing down his shaggy hair. She was glad to see it was back to normal. Marcus didn't look right all slicked back and buttoned up. "Why are you looking at me like that?"

"Oh, I…remembered that I found out the Blue Hills Theater is doing *A Midsummer Night's Dream* the day after Christmas. That's the place where my mom took me to see it a few years ago, and it made me want to be an actress. Maybe we could go together this time?" Lena was still curious about what Marcus was hiding, but she couldn't help getting excited as she told him about the performance. She'd actually squealed when she'd heard about it, accidentally waking Professor from a nap in the process.

She hoped Marcus would be excited too, but instead he said, "Oh...I don't know."

Lena swallowed her disappointment. "It's okay if you don't want to go. I know theater isn't your thing."

"If you like it, then of course it's my thing," he said, his amber eyes twinkling at her. "I might be doing stuff with my family that day, but maybe I can get out of it. I'll let you know, okay?"

Lena nodded, feeling a little better. Then Marcus started telling her how much he was enjoying the quilting book she'd lent him, and Lena's mood lightened. She couldn't believe he'd spend his free time reading about a hobby he wasn't even interested in. She couldn't imagine anyone else doing that for her, not even her best friends.

Whatever secret Marcus was keeping from her suddenly didn't seem so important. If he wasn't telling her about it, there had to be a good reason.

chapter 8

Marcus plopped down on the bleachers, scanning the indoor track for his sister. After a second, he spotted her doing some extreme leg stretches near the shot put area. He was shocked to see that she was talking and smiling with another girl on the team. Marcus wasn't used to his sister acting like an actual human.

Across the gym, Peter Chung and his new girlfriend were sitting so close together on the bleachers, they might as well have been welded together. The auras around them bled into each other, forming one blinding ball of light.

Marcus grinned. If he could get his sister's aura to be half that bright with whatever guy he found for her, he'd be happy. According to his matchmaking manual, a couple didn't always need to be zapped to fall in love. Sometimes, if two people spent enough time together, a love spark could ignite on its own. He only hoped he could convince his sister to give someone other than Peter a chance.

He sized up the guys on the track team, hoping one of them might be a good candidate. He had no idea what his sister looked for in a guy, but he figured anyone with a grayish aura like hers was a good place to start. He spotted one guy on the far end of the gym whose aura was pretty drab. He was short, probably about half of Ann-Marie's height. Maybe she'd be willing to overlook that? Then Marcus saw the guy picking his nose, right there in public, and he knew his sister would never go for it.

With a sigh, Marcus kept scanning until he spotted a guy sitting on his own in the corner. He was a loner like Ann-Marie. That was a good sign. The guy was pretending to tie and retie his shoe, but it was clear he was only trying to look busy so it wouldn't be obvious that he didn't have anyone to talk to. Marcus knew that move well. He'd done it plenty of times himself. When he squinted, he could see a hint of a gray aura around the guy's head. Good!

Marcus took out the dating book Grandpa had given him and started to flip through, trying to remember if there was any advice on handling shy people. There was no way his sister would make the first move, so he'd have to convince the guy to do it.

As he flipped to the "approaching the girl" section, a piece of paper fluttered out of the back of the book. He scooped it up, and his heart stopped as he recognized the handwriting on the piece of notepaper. It was Grandpa Joe's.

Marcus swallowed painfully. It had been almost two months since Marcus had had to guide his grandfather's soul to the After. He kept telling himself that missing Grandpa would get easier, but so far, his chest still ached whenever he thought about him. Even though Marcus knew that wherever he was now, Grandpa was okay, he still missed him constantly.

He took a deep breath and read the note.

> For my favorite grandson, so that you can "get the girl" the same way I got mine.
>
> Love always,
> Grandpa Joe.

Marcus stared at the words for a long time. Grandpa must have tucked the note into the back cover of the book when he'd given it to him, but somehow Marcus hadn't noticed it until now. How he wished he could talk to his grandfather and tell him that he *had* gotten the girl.

Slowly, Marcus slipped the note back into the book and snapped it shut. Maybe death wasn't as scary as he'd always thought—his time using Lena's powers had shown him that—but knowing that didn't make missing someone any easier. It didn't make Grandpa being gone seem any fairer.

He was about to get to his feet and flee when he heard a commotion from the track. A relay race was in progress, but the runners were stopping in confusion. In the middle of the track, two people were waltzing to music that only they seemed able to hear.

Wait. It was Peter and Claire!

They were completely oblivious, gazing into each other's eyes, as kids tried to pass batons around them. Meanwhile, people in the stands were shouting for them to get off the track.

Marcus jumped to his feet and ran down to the couple as they were dragged to the sidelines by a couple of angry coaches.

"Hey, I know you!" Peter called, pointing at Marcus. "You're Ann-Marie's little brother."

"Aw, he's adorable," Claire said. Then she turned to Peter. "But not as adorable as you, Sweetie Pie."

"You're the adorable one, Muffin Face!" Peter cooed back.

"No, you are, Chocolate Breath!" She grabbed his hand. "I feel like dancing some more! Come on!"

Marcus watched in fascinated horror as they tangoed out of the gym, the sparks around them flashing like strobe lights. What was going on? He'd seen plenty of couples in love, but this wasn't right. This was creepy!

When Marcus turned around, he found Ann-Marie staring

after the couple with a heartbroken expression on her face. He had never seen her aura so bleak before. How could Marcus ever succeed in fixing her up with someone else when it was obvious that she was still pining after Peter?

"Hey, Ann-Marie," he said. "Are you okay?"

"What did I say about you talking to people in my grade?" she demanded. "Why do you have to be such a freak?" Her voice broke, like she might start crying at any second. Then she turned with a squeak of her sneakers and marched toward the locker room.

Marcus hurried out of the gym and dialed Eddie's number. But when he explained what had happened, his boss didn't seem all that worried.

"Sometimes love jolts are particularly strong," he said. "This could be normal love behavior."

"I'm telling you, they were *waltzing* in the middle of the track during a race!" Marcus cried. "Kids were hurdling around them. That is not normal love stuff."

Eddie sighed, and there was a beep in the background like he was turning off his video game system. "Okay, I'll come test out your powers tonight. Chances are it's nothing to worry about."

But after Marcus hung up, he wasn't reassured. Whenever Eddie told him not to worry, it usually meant that things were about to get a whole lot worse.

chapter 9

Lena was on her way to play rehearsal when Eddie called with a new assignment. She tried to tell him that she couldn't be late, but Eddie only said, "You'll be done before you know it" and hung up the phone.

Lena was relieved when she realized the address was only a block away from school. Eddie was right. She should have plenty of time. Still, she'd been hoping to get to rehearsal early to talk to Mr. Jackson, maybe ask him to remind people to finally learn their lines.

As she walked into town, her thoughts went back to her amazing date with Marcus the other night. The allergic reaction and the slimy food had been small hiccups, but after dinner, she and Marcus had wandered around town holding hands and looking at all the Christmas decorations twinkling in people's yards. She'd floated home in a haze of happiness. She'd even dug up the "Things to Accomplish before I Turn Fourteen" list she'd made a while back and checked off "Perfect Date." Lena couldn't believe how much she'd already done on the list (First Kiss, First Boyfriend) and the school year wasn't even half over!

When she got to the address on her phone, Lena peered up at the deserted-looking building with "Watts Up Joke Shop" written in faded letters above the door. Was this really the place?

Lena glanced around at the empty street and then headed inside. The joke shop was covered in dust. She felt like she was breathing in mouthfuls of it, and there was a dry, stale smell in the air, as if the windows hadn't been opened in years.

After a couple minutes of wandering past shelves of whoopee cushions, snakes in a can, and tons of other cheesy joke gifts that she could imagine Marcus loving, Lena still hadn't found Mr. Franklin Watts, age seventy-four. Finally, she poked her head into the storeroom in the back and spotted him sleeping in a rickety chair by a wall of cardboard boxes. He was snoring so loudly, it was making the chair vibrate.

Good. Another sleeper. That would make things easier.

Her phone started beeping incessantly, telling her it was time. But when Lena called up her energy, nothing happened. She stared at her fingers and willed her energy to spark! Flare! Wake up!

Finally, her fingers started to glow—and then the purple light went out like a candle flame. What on earth?

Her phone beeped and beeped. She tried to get the energy

back into her hand again, but it was no use. Her power had disappeared.

She watched, wide-eyed, as Mr. Watts took his last breath and then, with a shuddering sigh, went still in his chair. The last of his snores echoed off the walls and fell silent.

Lena shook her hands and tried again. And again. "Come on!" she whispered. But no matter how hard she concentrated, there wasn't even a hint of a glow in her fingers.

When she squinted, she could see Mr. Watts's wisp of a soul detaching from his body. Without her zap, there would be nothing to send the soul into the After.

Lena stared as the light fluttered out of the old man's chest and into the air, drifting around like it was riding a gentle breeze. She tried to grab it, but her fingers went right through. All she could feel was the slightest hint of warmth. Then the soul drifted behind her and was gone.

She ran to the back door and threw it open, scanning the alley. Nothing. Panting, she sprinted back through the store and stumbled out onto the sidewalk. There was no sign of the ball of light.

Panic was pounding through her. She grabbed her phone and started to dial Eddie's number. But then she heard the faint sound of laughter echoing behind her.

Lena whirled to find the ball of light hanging in front of her face. She tried to grab it, but it backed away before she could make contact. She tried again, but again it evaded her. Almost like it was toying with her.

Then she heard another burst of laughter. It was definitely coming from the light. The soul *was* messing with her!

"Mr. Watts," she said, trying to calm herself down. Freaking out was not going to get the job done. "I know you must be scared about moving on, but I promise it'll be worth it. Come toward my hand, okay?"

For a second, it seemed like her words had worked. As she made her fingers flare again—this time, the glow was dull but steady—the ball of light drifted toward her. But when she went to grab it with her glowing hand, it zipped in between her ankles and dashed away.

"Mr. Watts! Wait!" she cried, chasing him out onto the street. Once again, she heard a faint laugh. It sounded like it was coming from the mailbox. She threw open the mail slot, and the ball of light shot at her like a swarm of bees. She gasped and stumbled backward, landing on the ground with a thump.

As she scrambled to her feet, her backside throbbing, the laugh came again, this time from above her head. Then she heard a faint voice say "Catch me if you can" before the light sped away down the street and disappeared behind a row of trash cans.

Lena stood paralyzed for a second, trying to decide what to do. Should she call Eddie for help? But this was her assignment, her mistake, and it was up to her to make it right. So she turned toward the spot where the soul had disappeared, and she ran.

chapter 10

Marcus rechecked the time on the oversized clock above Lena's mantel. It had been over four hours since his and Lena's powers had gone insane, and every minute that ticked by made him even more anxious.

"Eddie should be here by now," he said. Couldn't their boss at least be punctual when it was a real emergency?

"I can't believe I missed play rehearsal to chase a soul around!" Lena said, pacing in front of the living room window. "It was right there, and I let it go. If I could just—"

"Hey," Marcus gently cut in. "I know you want to keep looking for that soul on your own, but if something is wrong, then Eddie needs to know about it." Peter and Claire going gaga over each other might have been worrying, but Lena's powers fading out altogether was downright scary. What if that kind of thing started happening to Marcus's powers too?

Finally, the doorbell rang, and Eddie waltzed in carrying a scooter and a backpack. Marcus was momentarily disappointed at how ordinary the scooter was—so different from Eddie's usual tech toys—until he realized that the scooter was *part* of the backpack.

"Hey, kids," Eddie said, sliding the metal handle down until it disappeared into the fabric of the bag. "Wow, Marcus. That's quite the cologne you've got there! Trying to impress your special lady, huh?"

Marcus blushed even though Lena was still pacing around the room and didn't seem to hear. He'd been dousing himself with his dad's cologne ever since Lena had commented on it. It made his eyes feel like they were burning, but if Lena liked it, it was worth it.

"So what seems to be the problem?" Eddie asked.

"We think there might be something weird going on with our powers again," Lena said.

"I already told you about my match going overboard, and Lena's powers completely stopped working today," Marcus added.

Eddie turned toward Lena, absently wheeling his backpack back and forth by his feet. "Your assignment at the joke shop?"

"The soul got away. I tried to get it back when my powers started working again, but…" She shook her head.

"And did you notice anything odd before today?" Eddie asked.

Lena made a little sound in her throat. "I did have a hard time calling up my energy when I was with Natalie the other day," she said slowly. "I thought it was nerves, but maybe it was more than that."

"This isn't tied to our power swap, is it?" Marcus asked. "Because that happened weeks ago. Why would things suddenly get screwed up now?"

The two of them turned to watch Eddie scratching his short beard and muttering under his breath, like he was trying to work out a math equation. Finally, he said, "I want to try a test."

He had them stand side by side, and then he ordered Lena to hold out her hand and asked Marcus to call up his energy.

Marcus concentrated on his fingers, and almost instantly, they started glowing their usual red. "Looks fine to me," he said.

But then Eddie reached out and gave Lena's palm a quick pinch. "Ow!" she said.

The instant she cried out, Marcus's energy dimmed before going back to normal. "Whoa, what was that?"

Eddie didn't answer. Instead, he told Marcus to extinguish his energy and hold out his hand. Then he asked Lena to call up her energy.

"Why, so you can stomp on my foot?" Lena asked.

"Just go with it," Marcus told her. "I think Eddie's on to something."

"Fine," she said, calling up her energy. It was its usual deep purple.

Marcus prepared himself for a pinch, but it didn't come. Instead, Eddie leaned in and whispered in his ear: "Lena told Natalie that she doesn't really like you."

Marcus snapped his eyes up. "What?"

At the same moment, Lena gasped. "What did you do? My energy went out!"

Eddie edged backward until he was almost in the dining room. "Shoot. It's like I thought. Your powers are linked to each other's emotions." He looked at Marcus. "I apologize. What I just said isn't true. I was only trying to get a rise out of you to see if it would affect Lena's abilities."

Marcus gulped for air. Test or not, how could Eddie have said that to him? But if there was something wrong with their powers, he had to focus.

"But what kinds of emotions would mess up our powers so much?" Lena asked. "I wasn't upset or anything when Marcus zapped Peter. In fact, when we were at the bowling alley, I was really happy because I—" She smiled shyly. "I kept thinking how lucky I was to be there with Marcus."

He couldn't help the warmth that spread through his chest. He still couldn't get over the fact that Lena could feel the same way about him that he felt about her.

"Marcus, were you experiencing any strong emotions today when Lena was on her assignment?" Eddie asked.

The warmth in his chest faded. "Well, I did find a note from my grandpa. I guess that kind of messed me up."

Lena's face softened. "I'm sorry," she said, putting her hand on his shoulder. "Are you okay?"

Before he could answer, Eddie broke in. "This makes sense with my theory. Marcus, your match was overly strong because Lena's emotions were so positive, and Lena, your powers went out when Marcus was upset about the note."

"But why would that happen?" Marcus asked. "Everything seemed fine until a few days ago."

Eddie gave his earlobe a thoughtful tug. "After you two swapped powers, I was afraid there might be some lasting side effects. I believe your energies were imprinted on one other. Lena, that's why you can see auras the way Marcus can. And Marcus, that's why you're still able to see your ghost cat."

"What does that have to do with our powers not working?" Marcus asked.

"Because your energies are so closely linked, when you're in tune with each other, everything is fine. But when the two of you are on different frequencies, it can cause your powers to malfunction."

"What do you mean by 'different frequencies'?" Lena asked. "We're not radios!"

"When you're still emotionally connected but not necessarily in sync with each other."

"That doesn't make sense. Things have been going great between us," Marcus said. In fact, he'd never felt more in sync with someone, not even with Grandpa Joe.

Lena paced the room, rubbing her palm where Eddie had pinched it. "What are we supposed to do? I thought me being an emotionless robot was bad, but now feeling stuff is getting us into trouble!"

"Well, there is one simple solution." Eddie let out a long sigh, his face more serious than Marcus had ever seen it. "You two could end your relationship."

Marcus gawked at him. "Break up? Are you crazy?"

"Wait," Lena said. "You wouldn't suggest that unless things were really bad. Is this like before? Are our messed-up powers causing a chain reaction again?"

Oh no. Last time their powers had gone haywire, souls had gotten harder to catch and love matches had turned into hate matches. That couldn't happen again.

Lena gasped. "Wait, the haunted hospital! Is that because of us?" She turned to Marcus. "They were talking about it on the news. It's supposed to be the most haunted place in the country. I knew that sounded strange, especially because it's so close to us."

Eddie cleared his throat. "Let's not worry about that right now. I don't want to upset you any more than necessary."

"But telling us to break up is okay?" Marcus asked.

"I'm sorry, kid," Eddie said. "But the bond between you is unusually strong. Ending your relationship might be the best way to break it and sever the link between your emotions."

Marcus glanced at Lena, afraid that she might be looking convinced. But her mouth was in a tight, stubborn line. "No way," she said, and Marcus felt his shoulders relax. "You're going to have to find another way to fix this, because Marcus and I are fine right where we are."

"Then we will find another way," Eddie said, but his voice was full of doubt. "I'm afraid we're shorthanded right now, so I need you to keep working. You should still be able to do your assignments, but we have to be more careful about how you're feeling. In the meantime, I'll schedule a meeting with the boss lady to discuss the situation."

"But what if another soul wanders away because I accidentally slam my hand in a car door or something?" Marcus asked.

Eddie glanced at his watch and unfolded his scooter again. "I will try to figure out how to fix this," he said, inching toward the door. "In the meantime, stay calm and on good terms with each other."

"What about the soul that wandered away?" Lena asked.

"You should have reported that to me immediately." He gave her a disapproving finger wag. "Normally, I would send in a soul hunter, but I am short-staffed."

"So I can keep looking for it?" Lena asked, her face brightening.

"For now. Only until I find someone else for the job. We can't let souls wander too long or they become…unpredictable."

"What does that mean?" Marcus asked. The last thing they needed was Lena chasing down some crazed ghost. But Eddie had already breezed out the door and cruised into the night.

chapter 11

"Lena, what do you think about someone who's a deep-sea diver?" her dad asked as Lena rushed to get ready for school. "Is that plus two or minus two?"

Her dad was on the dating site again, going through his suggested matches while he sipped his morning coffee. He was treating the whole online dating thing like some kind of scientific problem. He'd even made a chart of people he thought he'd be most compatible with and given each of them a score based on their profile details. Apparently deep-sea diving didn't fit neatly into his formula.

Lena could imagine Marcus's reaction when he heard about the chart. He'd probably roll his eyes so hard, he'd hurt himself. She smiled at the thought and stuffed her foot into one of her sneakers.

Squilch.

Lena shrieked and yanked the shoe off. There was some kind of foam inside. It was white and thick and…minty? She leaned in and sniffed. Shaving cream. How on earth had shaving cream gotten into her shoe?

Professor padded over, ready to help clean it up with his tongue, but Lena shooed him away.

"Dad, have you gotten into practical jokes recently?" she called from the kitchen, scrubbing the inside of her shoe with a paper towel.

"That doesn't sound like me," he answered. "I'd probably give that a minus three." Clearly, his mind was still on the dating chart.

Suddenly, Lena thought she heard faint laughter behind her, but when she turned around, there was nothing there. She knew that laugh. Had Mr. Watts followed her home? She rushed from room to room, trying to find any hint of him, but he was long gone.

Defeated, she went back to the kitchen. Just her luck that her runaway soul was also a prankster. The sooner she sent him to the After, the better.

She shoved her mostly clean shoe back on, trying to avert her eyes as she passed by the playing card costume on the kitchen table. The half-finished monstrosity reminded Lena of the first quilt she'd ever made. It had been so lopsided and lumpy that she'd wound up giving it to Professor to chew on.

"Dad, I'll be home late today, okay?" she said, grabbing her backpack.

He glanced up from his laptop. "I thought you didn't have to be at rehearsal today."

"I don't, but…I said I'd help Marcus paint some sets." She hated lying to her dad, but she couldn't exactly tell him that she was going to track down a lost soul.

"You'll bring him by for dinner tomorrow?" His face lit up. "Maybe we can score him and see how you two chart."

"Don't you dare!" she said, but she couldn't help laughing. Then she gave her dad a peck on the check and rushed out the door, her foamy shoe squeaking with each step.

When Marcus got to the hockey rink that evening, he scanned the people filing in, searching for Peter Chung. According to his sister, Peter went to all the games, so he should be in attendance. Then Marcus could keep tabs on him and Claire and make sure that their super love boost didn't disrupt any more sporting events.

"Are you *stalking* me?" a voice asked behind him.

Marcus sighed as he turned to face his sister. "Can't I go to a game?"

Ann-Marie snorted. "You've never been to one before. You're not even dressed for it!"

Marcus realized she was right. He was the only one not wearing thick layers and a wool hat. He pulled his thin jacket tighter around him and said, "I'll be fine."

"Seriously, what are you doing here? And why do you reek of Dad's cologne?"

Ann-Marie looked ready to kick him out of the hockey rink altogether, but then she glanced past him, and the corners of her lips drooped, like she was biting the insides of her cheeks. Marcus knew that disappointed look. He'd seen it for days last year after his sister had missed out on getting the highest GPA in her grade by less than a point.

Sure enough, Peter Chung had walked in, hand in hand with Claire. The two of them were floating through the crowd, gazing into each other's eyes so deeply that they kept bumping into people.

"Whatever. Just stay away from me," Ann-Marie mumbled before rushing away.

Marcus went back to watching Peter and Claire, who were now doing some sort of weird dance in the doorway at the top of the stairs. When he got closer, he heard Peter saying, "No, after you," and Claire responding with, "No, really, after you." Marcus wondered how many hours they'd spent in doorways like this since he'd zapped them.

Finally, he couldn't take it anymore. He went over and

yanked open the other half of the double door so they could both fit through at the same time.

"Thanks!" Peter said. Then he did a double take. "Oh, hey, Marcus. Is your sister here?" He scanned the crowd as if hoping to find her.

Before Marcus could answer, Claire let out an impatient sigh. "Doughnut Cheeks, the game's starting!"

At the sound of her voice, Peter seemed to forget he was in the middle of a conversation. He grabbed Claire's hand again, and together they pranced down to their seats. Marcus nearly choked when he saw them sit down directly in front of Ann-Marie. His sister now had a front-row seat to their lovefest.

When Marcus plopped down next to Ann-Marie, she jumped at the sight of him. "Why are you sitting with me?" she hissed.

"Are we supposed to pretend we don't know each other?"

"Yes," she said, turning away.

At that moment, Marcus's dad glanced up from his spot by the team bench, as if looking for his daughter. When he and Marcus locked eyes, his dad's mouth sagged open. Then he smiled and waved, looking genuinely glad to see him. Marcus waved back, feeling a little guilty that this was the first time he'd ever been to a game, considering that his dad had been coaching the team for years.

Ann-Marie groaned. "Seriously, go away. You're embarrassing me."

"I'm not doing anything."

What he was actually doing was watching Peter and Claire out of the corner of his eye. So far, they weren't paying any attention to the game. Marcus kept waiting for them to talk, but they simply sat in absolute silence, eyes locked in some kind of lovey-dovey staring contest. When he squinted, he saw that their auras were still blurred together and blindingly bright, but the sparks were different now. They were intense in color, but they weren't bouncing around anymore. Instead, they were meandering around, looking tired and—if Marcus had to put a name to it—bored. Could love sparks *be* bored?

Marcus racked his brain. What did all this mean? He'd been assigned to zap these two after all. Weren't they supposed to be a good pair? But then he remembered what his matchmaking manual said about short-lived romances. Sometimes a love boost was only supposed to be temporary. Summer romances, for example, were meant to fade. Maybe Peter and Claire were only supposed to have a little fling and then get over each other, but because of his too-strong zap, now they were stuck together even though they weren't a perfect match. It didn't even seem like they had anything to talk about!

Meanwhile, Ann-Marie's aura was as drab as ever as she

watched the couple canoodling in front of her. If only Marcus could find someone else for her.

He scanned the crowd and finally spotted a guy sitting a few rows ahead who had a gray aura around his head. Marcus was pretty sure it was the same guy he'd seen retying his shoes at the track meet.

"Hey, do you know him?" Marcus asked, pointing.

"Albert Landry?" she said. "What about him?"

"Oh, um. I was talking to him earlier, and he seemed like a nice guy. He had lots of good things to say about you too."

Ann-Marie rolled her eyes. "I doubt it. He's the one who beat me out for highest GPA last year, but I'm already two whole points ahead of him this year. He's going to hate me when he finds out."

Marcus sighed. So much for that idea.

After the first period of the game ended, Claire snapped her gaze away from Peter and announced that she was getting some hot chocolate. "Do you want me to get you some, Dimple Toes?"

Peter nodded slowly and watched her walk away as if he might never see her again. Marcus actually expected him to burst into song. When she faded from sight though, Peter's mind seemed to clear a little. He glanced behind him, and his face lit up.

"Oh, hey," he said to Ann-Marie. "How's the game going so far? I'm having a hard time paying attention for some reason."

Ann-Marie flashed a stiff smile and started to give him a play-by-play. The more they talked though, the more at ease they seemed with each other. After a couple of minutes, they were giggling over some hockey stuff that Marcus didn't understand. He couldn't help noticing how happy his sister looked. Her face was glowing like she was the one who'd gotten a love boost.

When he glanced around to check if Claire was on her way back—he kind of hoped she'd stay away forever—he caught sight of a familiar face on the other side of the ice. Lena's new friend Natalie was leaning against a railing, scribbling in a green notebook. She glanced up, and her eyes immediately locked on his, almost as if she'd been staring at him moments earlier. Quickly, Natalie turned away, shoved her notebook in her bag, and hurried off.

Marcus frowned. That was weird.

Claire returned holding two cups of hot chocolate and slipped one into Peter's hand with an adoring coo. He gave Ann-Marie an apologetic smile and said, "Well, see ya." Then he went back to silently mooning over his new girlfriend.

Marcus expected his sister to wilt like one of the prize roses she grew in their backyard, so he was surprised to catch her smiling to herself. And after their team scored a goal, Peter snapped out of his stupor for a second and gave Ann-Marie a knowing look over his shoulder.

When he saw their little exchange, Marcus sat up straight, bubbling with excitement. Maybe there was hope for Ann-Marie and Peter after all.

chapter 12

The joke shop seemed even dustier than it had the day before, but Lena covered her nose and started scanning the place for any hint of Mr. Watts's soul. According to her manual, souls tended to stay near places that they knew or felt comfortable. That's why even though Marcus's ghost cat hadn't known him when it was alive, it hung around Marcus's house now because it felt safe there. Lena wished her manual had more info on tracking souls down, but she supposed she'd need a soul hunter manual for that. Lena hadn't given it much thought before, but being a soul hunter actually sounded pretty interesting. There was something exciting about the "thrill of the hunt."

"Mr. Watts?" she called softly as she wandered down an entire aisle of rubber chickens. "I know you've been following me around. Thanks for the shaving cream in my shoe this morning. Really funny."

She kept scanning the aisles, but there was no sign of him.

Finally, she found a small desk in the back of the store. There were utility bills crammed into every corner and scraps of paper with scrawled notes on them that made no sense: "Two ducks waddle into a bar" and "The difference between an egg and a watermelon."

Lena realized that they sounded like the setups for jokes, which made more sense when she saw a few old newspaper clippings about comedy shows that Mr. Watts had done when he was younger. Apparently, he used to be a stand-up comedian before he opened a joke shop.

Suddenly, Lena heard footsteps in the back room. It couldn't be Mr. Watts. Balls of light didn't have feet. Then again, balls of light shouldn't be able to spray shaving cream in people's shoes.

Lena crept toward the door and peered inside. She found a petite woman, probably a little younger than Lena's dad, pacing the length of the back room. Before Lena could duck back out and make a run for it, the woman stopped pacing and gave Lena a startled look.

"I'm sorry," she said. "The door was unlocked, so I let myself in. Am I not supposed to be here?"

"No, it's okay," Lena said. Clearly, this woman thought she worked here or something. Then she did a double take, realizing she knew her. "You're my aunt Teresa's friend, right? Viv?"

The woman blinked. "Little Lena Perris, is that you? You're all grown up! How's your aunt doing? I haven't seen her in ages!"

"She's good," Lena said. "Um, are you okay?"

Viv dabbed at her eyes with a tissue. "When I heard the news about Watts, I didn't know where else to go." She let out a sound between a sob and a laugh. "My jokes are such a mess, and I have a gig this weekend. Normally I'd come here to run them by Watts, but…"

"I'm sorry," Lena said. "If it helps, I, um, heard he went peacefully in his sleep." This was technically true, even though his soul wasn't anywhere near at peace yet.

Viv staggered over to a chair and sank down into it, only to instantly jump up when a loud farting sound echoed through the store. Sure enough, there was a whoopee cushion on the seat.

"Typical Watts," Viv said with a sad chuckle.

Lena's ears perked up. She thought she'd heard a faint laugh coming from behind her. Was it possible Mr. Watts was still here? If she could get him to laugh again, she might be able to figure out where he was.

He obviously enjoyed it when people looked ridiculous, so Lena grabbed a pile of fake dog poop from a nearby table and stuck it on her head. Viv looked at her like she was insane, but

Lena heard the laugh again. It was coming from near a stack of boxes marked "Fart Powder."

"How did you know Mr. Watts?" Lena asked, inching toward the boxes.

"I am—was—in his stand-up classes. He taught me how to be funny when everyone else said I was hopeless."

"I thought that wasn't the kind of thing you could teach," Lena said, remembering what Mr. Jackson had once said about Abigail's "natural comedic timing."

Viv began wandering around the stacks of boxes until she was practically hidden among them. "Watts said you couldn't teach a piece of wood to be funny because it had no emotions, but if a person feels things, that person can do comedy. And he was right. I used to be—"

Lena didn't hear the rest. At that moment, she saw the ball of light hovering near a set of shelves. She lunged, trying to call up her energy, but her fingers only flared once and went out. She felt the warmth of the soul zip past her fingers before it disappeared out the window.

"Gah!" Lena cried. She'd almost had it! Whatever Marcus was feeling at that moment must have messed up her powers again.

"Are you okay?" Viv asked, peering around a box of fake mustaches.

Just then, Lena's hand flared up purple again, all on its own. She quickly hid it behind her back. Had Viv seen? If Lena's powers were working properly, other people shouldn't notice anything strange, but the normal rules didn't seem to apply anymore.

"Lena? Is everything all right?" Viv asked. Thankfully, it didn't seem like she'd noticed the glowing fingers.

"I have to go," Lena said. Then she stopped. "Actually, do you know where Mr. Watts lived?" Maybe his soul bounced around between there and here.

Viv nodded and gave her an address. "It's right next to the Laundromat." She sniffed. "Watts always said that thanks to that place, he hated the smell of clean clothes. He'd joke about throwing dirt on his shirts the minute he took them out of the dryer." She started to cry softly.

"Is there anything I can do?" Lena felt bad leaving her like this.

Viv shook her head. "I'll be okay. Tell your aunt I say hi."

Lena hovered for another minute, still unsure. Finally, Viv waved her away, insisting she was fine.

"Don't worry. Everything is going to be okay," Lena said lamely. Then she rushed out the door and pulled her phone out of her pocket. She called Marcus, but it went straight to voice mail. Maybe he was still at the hockey game. Whatever he was doing, it was clearly making him feel all sorts of things.

She'd always liked how Marcus was so much more sensitive than other guys their age, but for once, she wished he could feel things a little less deeply. Then maybe there wouldn't be a lost soul wandering around, getting more and more out of control.

chapter 13

M arcus!" his mom called. "You have a guest."

Marcus jumped up from his worktable, the familiar panic washing over him. He never had people over to his house. Even though it wasn't a total shrine to Ann-Marie's track accomplishments anymore and his mom had been making slightly less smelly art projects in the basement recently, it was still an embarrassing mess.

When he saw Lena standing in the doorway, he relaxed for a second. She was the only person he'd ever trusted to see the inside of his house. But the look on her face told him that something was wrong.

"Remember that it's a school night," his mom said. But then she gave him a little wink and headed back to her studio.

"Marcus, did something happen at the hockey game tonight?" Lena asked, dragging him outside onto the porch. "Is that why my powers were going nuts again?"

"Whoa, slow down." He shut the door to the house and

waved her over to the swing, even though it was a cold night. He didn't want his family to overhear. "What's going on?"

As Lena told him about losing the soul at the joke shop, she furiously paced around the porch. "So?" she asked when she was done. "Were your emotions off or anything?"

Marcus thought it over, trying to put what he'd been feeling into words. "When I first got to the game, I was confused about Peter and Claire. And then it seemed like fixing my sister up with someone else was hopeless. But then it turned out Peter and Ann-Marie might be a good match after all, if I can figure out how to get Claire out of the picture."

"So your emotions were all over the place, just like my powers," Lena said, plopping down beside him. "I hate this! Everything feels so out of control!"

"Lena, it's okay," he said, putting his arm around her. "We'll make some rules, that's all. Next time one of us has an assignment or is doing anything with our powers, we'll text each other and make sure we're calm and relaxed."

"But what if we can't do that? What if—"

"I'll ask my sister for some stretches," he said. "Stuff to calm us down. She was really into yoga last year. Maybe that would help."

Lena let out a long sigh. "I bet my dad could recommend some scientifically proven relaxation techniques."

"And Eddie's working to fix this, so it won't be forever."

"You're right," Lena said, giving him a weak smile. "I've just never messed up this badly before."

Marcus smiled back. He could relate. "I was actually wishing one of my matches would break up today, even though that would end my perfect matchmaking streak," he said. "I guess we're both a little off. But we'll get back on track, okay?"

"You always know what to say to make me feel better." She bumped his elbow with hers. "Have I mentioned how awesome you are?"

Marcus felt his ears get hot. "You might have, but it's always nice to hear it." He didn't know what Eddie had been talking about when he'd said the two of them weren't in tune with each other.

"Okay, so the plan is that we don't let things rattle us." Lena laughed. "I used to be great at that. This should be easy!"

He wasn't sure "easy" was the right word, but as long as their lives stayed calm from now on, everything should be okay.

chapter 14

Marcus was on his way to lunch when Caspar Brown cornered him in the hallway. Marcus's instinct was to run, but he told his feet to stay put. He wasn't afraid of Caspar anymore, he reminded himself.

"Hey, I liked what you did with that space station," Caspar said. Since he barely opened his mouth when he talked, all his words came out sounding more like grunts. "Someone said you have an old space robot too, the kind with the long metal arms?"

Marcus swallowed. He hadn't wanted to believe that the guy who'd spent months torturing him was now willing to pay him for his models, but Marcus also hadn't been able to turn down the offer, not when he had Lena's Christmas present to save up for. But the robot was different.

"That one's not for sale." He couldn't get rid of it, no matter how much he wanted to impress Lena.

"Fine," Caspar said, puffing air through his nose like a bull.

"Let me know if you change your mind." Then he ambled away, probably off to give some unsuspecting sixth grader a wedgie.

Marcus slipped into the cafeteria and headed toward Lena's table. He couldn't wait until he had enough money to buy tickets to see *A Midsummer Night's Dream* at the Blue Hills Theater. When Lena had brought up the idea of going together, he hadn't known what to say. "I don't want to get tickets with you, because I'm planning to get them for you for Christmas?" He could tell she'd been disappointed by his reaction, but he hoped she'd forget about all of that once he gave her the present.

As Marcus sat down at Lena's lunch table, he wasn't surprised to hear Hayleigh talking about Emery Higgins yet again.

"You're sure he didn't say anything about liking someone in the play?" Hayleigh was grilling Abigail. "That's what Connie Reynolds said."

Abigail groaned. "I told you, Emery barely ever talks! For all I know, he has crushes on everyone."

"Maybe we should go ask Connie," Hayleigh said, already getting to her feet. "Come on." Then, despite Abigail's objections, Hayleigh dragged her off to the far end of the cafeteria where Connie Reynolds was holding court at the popular kids' table.

"Emery *is* kind of cute," Natalie chimed in, looking up from the green notebook that she had tucked in her lap. "Even with the braces."

Marcus squinted across the cafeteria to where Emery and Justin Alvarez were tossing French fries across the table at each other. For a second, Marcus thought he saw a hint of a gray aura around Emery's head, almost like he was meant to get a love boost soon. But when Marcus looked again, it was gone. He must have imagined it.

Lena laughed. "I'm pretty sure the braces are how Emery got cast as the Cheshire Cat. He totally looks the part."

"I was the Cheshire Cat a couple years ago!" Natalie said. "They painted my whole face so it looked like I had nothing but teeth!" She let out a chirping laugh that sounded oddly fake. Marcus couldn't help wondering if she was always this cheerful.

"I didn't know you liked acting," Lena said.

"I'm not that good, but I love doing plays! It's so much fun!" Natalie turned to Marcus. "Don't you think so? Lena said you're helping out with the sets for *Alice*."

Marcus coughed. Honestly, he was dreading having to go back to the theater and paint more trees. How much shrubbery could possibly fit on a single stage? But painting sets was way better than watching videos of old plays. Lena had already forced him to sit through a recording of last year's school play.

He didn't remember much of it, mostly because his eyes had kept closing by themselves throughout the whole thing. But if that was the kind of stuff she liked to do, then he would have to suffer through it.

"So I saw you at the hockey game last night," he said, trying to change the subject.

Natalie gave him a blank look. "Hockey game?"

"Yeah, I was on the opposite side of the rink. I could tell it was you because you had that notebook with you."

Natalie let out a soft laugh. "Sorry, it must have been someone else." Then she quickly tucked the notebook in her bag as if she didn't want him to see it.

Um. Okay. Why would she lie about something like that? But he didn't press. Instead, he asked, "So where did you move from?"

"A few states over," Natalie said. Marcus waited for her to go on, but she was busy taking a bite of her sandwich.

"And Lena said you live in my neighborhood on Maple Street? Which house?"

Natalie let out the chirping laugh again. "I know this sounds silly, but I don't know my new address yet! It's the white one though."

Marcus raised an eyebrow. About half the houses on Maple Street were white. Was he imagining things, or was Natalie purposely dodging his questions? Then again, she barely knew him. Maybe his questions were too personal or something.

"Have you done any soul-collecting assignments on your own yet?" he asked, figuring their jobs were a safe topic. "Eddie couldn't wait to start sending me out every chance he got."

"Nope, not yet!" She jammed another bite of sandwich into her mouth and then gulped down some water, almost like she was avoiding having to say anything else.

Marcus glanced at Lena, wondering if she was noticing this too, but she seemed distracted by someone who had come into the cafeteria with the vice principal. It was a woman Marcus was pretty sure he'd never seen before, but there was something familiar about her.

"Lena, are you okay?" Marcus asked as Lena slowly got to her feet.

"I…I'll be right back."

"What's going on? Who is that?"

Lena gave him a dazed look. "It's my mom."

Lena felt like she was floating across the cafeteria. What was her mom doing here? When she'd first seen her come in with the vice principal, Lena had hardly recognized her. Her hair was much shorter and sleeker than it had been a year ago, and her face didn't have that too-angular look to it anymore. In fact, she barely seemed like the person she'd been last Christmas.

"Ah, Lena, there you are," the vice principal said. "Your mother and I were trying to find you."

"What…what's going on?" Lena's arms dangled awkwardly at her sides. She never knew if she should hug her mom when she saw her. "Is Grandma okay?"

"Everything's fine," her mom said. "I wanted to come surprise you, that's all. My flight got in early."

"Three weeks early?" The last she'd heard, her mom wasn't going to be in town until Christmas Eve.

Her mom gently put her hand on Lena's shoulder. "I couldn't wait to see you." She gave the vice principal a bright smile. "Do you mind if my daughter and I have some time to chat? I'll make sure she gets to her next class on time."

"Of course," he said. "You can go out into that hallway. It should be quiet this time of day."

Lena's mom grabbed her hand and led her out of the cafeteria. Her warm fingers suddenly transported Lena back to when she was little, back to when she thought her mom could do no wrong. Well, she knew better now. Lena snatched her hand away and shoved it into her pocket.

As the cafeteria door shut behind them, the booming sounds of eighth-grade lunch faded, and Lena could hear her own pulse pounding in her ears. This didn't make sense. Her mom never came into town unannounced, and she knew how much Lena hated surprises.

"Mom, really, what are you doing here?"

"Isn't it enough that I missed you?" her mom asked, wrinkles popping up around her dark eyes.

Lena didn't know how to answer that. If her mom missed her so much, why did she stay away for ninety-nine percent of the year?

"Come sit with me," her mom said, leading her over to a bench next to a display case full of old town maps. "We have so much catching up to do. Your father told me you have a boyfriend now!"

"You called Dad?" Her parents almost never talked on the phone. Mostly they sent messages to each other through Lena's grandmother.

"I spoke to him this morning to let him know I was coming to see you. He also said you got into the school play. Congratulations! Ever since we went to that Shakespeare festival, you've had the acting bug. I knew you'd eventually catch it from me."

"From you?" Lena asked. "I don't remember you doing any acting."

Her mom looked at her in surprise. "I used to do plays all

the time! Of course, it was only community theater, but I loved it. I'd bring you to rehearsals sometimes, and you'd sit on the edge of the stage and watch us." She smiled at the memory. "I'm sure you remember that!"

Lena shook her head. It felt like her mom was talking about a total stranger.

Her mom's smile faded. "Well, I suppose the last time I was in a play, you were about three years old. It makes sense that you wouldn't remember. After that, I was too busy to try out for things anymore."

A thick silence fell between them. Lena didn't know what to say. How could you catch up on an entire year in a few minutes?

"Listen, honey." Her mom's face grew serious, and suddenly her cheeks looked a little too hollow again. "I came back because I have something to ask you, and I didn't want to wait any longer."

Lena held her breath. Here it was, whatever bad news her mom had come all this way to tell her.

Her mom turned to her, her eyes suddenly shining with excitement. "I want you to come out to Arizona and live with me!"

chapter 15

As Marcus waited for Lena to come back to the cafeteria, his phone rang.

It was Eddie. That was weird. Eddie never called during school. One of the things they'd agreed on when Marcus had become a matchmaker was that his supernatural life wouldn't interfere with his school life.

"Um, hello?" he said softly, hiding the phone with his hand since using it during school hours was technically not allowed. He was glad Abigail and Hayleigh still hadn't come back from cross-examining Connie Reynolds, so at least he didn't have to hide his conversation from them.

"Marcus, I have an assignment for you," Eddie said.

"Now?"

Eddie chuckled. "I know this is a little unusual, kid, but you'll understand in a minute." Then he hung up.

Marcus waited impatiently for the assignment info to appear on his phone. When it came, he laughed.

"Is everything okay?" Natalie asked.

Marcus had forgotten she was sitting only a few feet away from him. He was about to lie and tell Natalie it was nothing, but then he remembered that he could actually be honest with her about his secret identity. "I'm supposed to fix up Emery Higgins."

"No way! Who with?"

"No idea," Marcus said. "I never know the target until I've made the match." He glanced at Emery across the cafeteria, and sure enough, the aura around him was back. Marcus hadn't imagined it after all. He had twelve minutes left until the match, just enough time to finish his lunch and make up an excuse to go talk to Emery.

But wait. He had to let Lena know so she could do the deep breathing exercises her dad had said were scientifically proven to help during times of emotional distress. He texted her, warning her that he was about to do an assignment, and then waited to hear back. Nothing.

"Are you okay?" Natalie asked after a minute.

Marcus realized he was tearing his napkin into strips. He jumped to his feet and poked his head out into the hallway where Lena had disappeared, but it was empty. He glanced at his phone. Five minutes until his match. He sent her another message.

Where are you? Are you calm? Are you doing your breathing?

Still no answer. He was almost out of time. And if he didn't do his match at the right moment, the balance of the universe would be thrown off. That had to be worse than risking having his powers be too strong again, right?

He didn't have time to call Eddie and ask him. Instead, he rushed back into the cafeteria and hurried to where Emery was sitting. It was only two tables over from where Abigail and Hayleigh were hanging out, probably still grilling Connie about who Emery had a crush on. Marcus hoped they were doing it in actual whispers and not stage whispers, so as not to completely terrify the poor guy. Maybe Hayleigh would finally get her wish, and Emery would be matched with her.

"Emery!" Marcus said, hurrying up to him. "Um, I had a question about the play."

"Yeah?" he said, his braces glittering under the fluorescent lights.

"Um. Do you know how many trees are in the first scene you're in? I'm, um, trying to count how many we need to paint."

"Oh." Emery wrinkled his nose in concentration. "Five, maybe? I'm not sure. You should ask Mr. Jackson."

Marcus's phone started beeping in his pocket. It was time.

He drew in a deep breath and willed his energy to spark. He could feel his fingers flare to life.

"Good idea. Thanks, Emery!" Marcus said, going to clap him on the back. But when Marcus lifted his hand, something strange happened. The light sputtered for a moment and then his fingers started spraying sparks all over the place like a lawn sprinkler.

He watched in horror as the sparks not only showered Emery, but also two people who were walking by. People who happened to be Abigail and Hayleigh.

All three of them froze as if they'd been stunned. And then the two girls looked at Emery, their expressions far-off and moony.

Uh oh.

"Hi, Emery," Abigail and Hayleigh cooed in unison.

"Hi," he said, grinning from ear to ear, Cheshire Cat style. "You both look great today. Just great."

Oh no!

"Thank you!" they both squealed. And then they turned to each other, glaring.

"Hey," Hayleigh said, trying to elbow in front of Abigail. "Do you mind? I'm talking to Emery."

"Do *you* mind?" Abigail shot back. "I was talking to him first."

Meanwhile, Emery was gazing between them like he'd never seen such beautiful creatures.

Oh no, oh no, oh no! Marcus could plainly see sparks bouncing between Abigail and Emery *and* between Hayleigh and Emery. As far as he could tell, the sparks on either side were exactly the same, meaning the connections were equally strong. What was he supposed to do?

And where was Lena? Whatever she was feeling right now, it couldn't be good. Not if it had caused her two closest friends to fall for the same guy.

chapter 16

Lena's head was throbbing as she grabbed a bag of sour cream and onion potato chips from the emergency stash her dad kept above the fridge. She couldn't believe her mom had shown up out of the blue and asked her to drop everything and run off to Arizona!

It was a good thing Mr. Jackson hadn't needed Lena at play rehearsal that afternoon. She didn't think she could spend a single minute playing a game of tag in character or brainstorming her character's favorite type of cake. Mr. Jackson was already mad at her for missing rehearsal the day before. She was sure he'd be even more annoyed if she lost her composure and announced that playing cards couldn't eat cake because they didn't have *mouths*.

She knew she should be out hunting for Mr. Watts's soul, but instead, Lena found herself looking over her "Things to Accomplish Before I Turn Fourteen" checklist again. Nowhere on that list did it say anything about her mom. Lena had given up on her years ago.

And yet, her mom claimed to have changed. In some ways, she did seem different. When she'd talked about her new nursing job and her new apartment, she'd radiated with happiness in a way Lena had never seen before.

Once Lena polished off the entire bag of potato chips, she not only felt queasy, but she was breathing onion fire. She sighed and went to the bathroom to brush her teeth. The instant she put the toothbrush in her mouth, she screamed and spit it back out. Her entire mouth was burning with the taste of salt!

For a second, she heard faint laughter behind her. Then it disappeared.

Gah! She poured mouthwash into her mouth and frantically swished it around, but the taste of salt was still lurking in the back of her throat. She knew better than to go chasing around the house again. Mr. Watts was certainly long gone by now.

This must have been what Eddie meant when he said lost souls became unpredictable. Of course, Mr. Watts wouldn't want to move on to the After when he was having so much fun driving Lena insane.

The doorbell rang, making her jump. Professor started bounding around the house as it rang a few more times. Whoever was outside clearly wasn't leaving.

She went to open the door and froze. What if this was

another practical joke? What if she opened the door and wound up with a bucket of water on her head?

Very carefully, she inched the door open, ready to slam it shut again. She let out a long breath when she found Natalie on her doorstep.

"Oh good. It's you," Lena said, pulling the door open all the way.

"Hey, I came by to bring you these." Natalie held up the books that Lena hadn't even remembered leaving in the cafeteria.

"Thanks," she said. Would it be rude to grab the books and not invite Natalie inside?

"Marcus was worried when you didn't come back at lunch," Natalie said, leaning against the door frame. Clearly, she wasn't going anywhere.

Lena sighed. "I saw him after school. He told me about Abigail and Hayleigh." She couldn't believe her emotions about her mom coming back had caused such a mess! But when Marcus had asked her about it, she'd simply told him that her mom was in town for a couple of days and that the shock of seeing her must have made his powers go haywire. Lena couldn't tell him—or anyone else—about her mom's proposal, even if she wasn't actually considering it. She could imagine what would happen: her dad would try to be a little too supportive, Marcus would freak out at the very idea, and her friends would probably yell at her for even speaking to her mom again.

When Marcus had called Eddie to tell him about the Emery/Abigail/Hayleigh situation, their boss had only sighed and said it would wear off in time and to be more careful. Not exactly the most helpful advice when Lena had seen Abigail and Hayleigh practically tearing Emery's limbs out this afternoon as they fought over who'd get to walk him to seventh period. And in a way, it was all her fault.

"Are you okay?" Natalie asked. "Marcus said you must have been pretty upset for his powers to get so crazy."

Lena started to say she was fine, but then she realized that Natalie didn't know her mom or care about the idea of her moving away. Maybe she was exactly the kind of person Lena could talk to. And she needed to talk to someone. What had happened with her mom was too big and bubbling for her to hold in much longer.

She led Natalie into the living room, filling her in on how her mom had left years ago on Valentine's Day and how frosty things had been between them ever since—until today when she'd waltzed back into Lena's life.

"Can you imagine me going to live with her?" Lena asked when she was done. "She doesn't know anything about me. It would be a disaster. But when I tried to tell her that, she said I shouldn't make up my mind yet."

"If you lived with her, you guys would get to know each other again," Natalie pointed out.

Lena gawked at her. "Are you saying I should go with her?"

"I'm saying…in my family, it's my dad and me who don't see each other. If I had a chance to fix things with him, I'd take it." Her voice suddenly sounded a lot less perky than usual.

Lena looked at her in surprise, realizing that she didn't know anything about Natalie's family. She'd assumed she lived with both her parents. "What happened with your dad?"

"My mom had me when she was pretty young, and my dad didn't even know I existed for a while, so…" Natalie shrugged. "There's a chance your mom really does want to reconnect with you."

As much as Lena didn't want to admit it, maybe Natalie was right. Her mom *had* seemed genuinely excited about the idea of Lena coming to live with her. "But how am I supposed to leave everyone behind? My dad would be miserable without me!"

"You wouldn't have to go forever."

That was true. Her mom had said she could wait until the end of the fall term, or even until the end of the school year. "I guess I could visit for a week or two, maybe over winter vacation," she said slowly. "See if I like it."

"There you go!" Natalie said, beaming at her like Lena had solved a huge math problem all on her own. "Did you tell Marcus about your mom's offer?"

"Not yet. I'm afraid he won't take it very well."

"Of course he won't. He really likes you." Natalie chewed on her lip. "Maybe..."

"What?" Lena asked when she didn't go on.

"Well, it's none of my business, but maybe you shouldn't tell him you're thinking of leaving until you make up your mind. My ex-boyfriend kind of freaked out when I told him I was moving here. He didn't want to even try to stay together, said it would be too hard."

Lena felt strange at the thought of keeping something so big from Marcus for much longer. Could she really not mention it when he came over for dinner that night? But Natalie had a point. Things were going so well between her and Marcus. Maybe it would be better to enjoy them for now and not worry about something that might not even happen.

Instead, she needed to focus on dealing with the things that were happening right now. She didn't want to spend even one more day worrying about buckets of water—or worse—falling on her head every time she opened a door.

chapter 17

Marcus hovered outside the indoor track building, scanning the crowd for Peter Chung. His hands were so sweaty that he worried about the box of chocolates he was holding. What if they melted before he managed to deliver them? He doubted Peter would be all that impressed with a box full of chocolate soup.

Finally, he spotted Peter rounding the corner. For once, he was alone. As Marcus had hoped, Claire was still at cheerleading practice.

"Hey, Peter!" Marcus said, rushing up to him before he could chicken out. His sister would murder him if she found out what he was about to do, but he couldn't think about that now. "I have something for you."

"Oh, okay," Peter said, clearly surprised.

Marcus thrust the box of chocolates at him. "Here," he said. "From a secret admirer." He felt silly saying the words, but that's what Grandpa's dating book had advised. *Woo your sweetheart with mystery chocolates and flowers!* Later, you were supposed to reveal that the gifts were from you, and the person was supposed to melt in your arms.

"Wow, thanks," Peter said. He opened the package and smiled. "Dark chocolate. My favorite."

Marcus sighed in relief. He'd had an inkling that Peter would like dark chocolate—maybe it was his matchmaking intuition—and the chocolates were still mostly intact.

"Claire knows me so well!" Peter added.

Marcus's mouth sagged open. "Oh, um... Actually, they're from my—"

But Peter wasn't listening. He was gulping down the chocolates by the handful, almost like he couldn't stop himself. "I love these!" he mumbled. "I love her! I love life! I have to go tell her right now!" Then he jammed one last handful into his mouth and gave Marcus a sugary grin before he pranced away toward the gym where Claire would no doubt melt into his chocolate-smeared arms.

When Lena got to Mr. Watts's apartment, she could tell it was the right place. Not only was it above a Laundromat like Viv had said, but the front doormat said "Ouch! Get off of me!" instead of "Welcome." She was willing to bet the joke shop sold them.

She glanced around and then tried the door, surprised when it opened. Maybe because she was still technically on assignment, all the same rules applied. She quickly slipped inside and closed the door behind her.

Lena expected the apartment to be as dusty and cluttered as the joke shop, but it was actually pretty airy and neat. It looked like Mr. Watts had spent very little time there, in fact. That meant it was unlikely that his soul would be hanging around. Still, she wandered through the small rooms just in case, but the only mildly interesting things she found were old playbills from a bunch of local theater productions that had happened before Lena's parents were even born. Apparently, before he'd become a comedian and a joke shop owner, Mr. Watts had also done some acting.

Disappointed with her search, Lena was about to leave when she heard someone struggling to open the front door. She considered trying to climb out the window, but it was too late. The door was already swinging open.

She tried to look casual, as if she belonged there, but she knew she was in trouble. Then she saw Viv come through the door, and relief washed over her. Maybe she could get away without anyone calling the police after all.

"Lena!" Viv said, frowning. "What are you doing here?"

"Tying up some loose ends," Lena said slowly. "I was just leaving though."

"No, don't go!" Viv let out a dry laugh. "Watts didn't have any family, so I volunteered to start sorting through his things. But now I'm not so sure I can handle it on my own."

"Sorry, I have to get home, and it's going to take me a while to ride my bike back." This part was true at least. Tonight was the big meeting between her dad and Marcus.

"I'll drive you," Viv said. "Please. It would be so helpful to go through his things with someone else who knew him. And you can fill me in on what your aunt Teresa's been up to recently."

Lena swallowed. She didn't want to keep lying to Viv, but she'd feel even worse abandoning her when she clearly didn't want to be alone. "I guess I could stay for a few minutes."

As they started going through closets, Lena felt even guiltier for touching a total stranger's things. But Viv seemed to need someone to talk to. She reminisced about the first time she met Watts and how he'd helped her find joy in life again after her messy divorce. "He said something that's helped me through the rough times," Viv said as she boxed up some musty sweaters. "He told me, 'Hon, you need to find the fun in life and hold on to it.' And he was right."

The more she talked, the more Lena liked her and the worse

she felt about lying to her, especially when Viv asked her how long she'd known Watts.

"Not long," Lena said, choosing her words carefully. "I only met him pretty recently through work."

Viv nodded. "He'd been talking about hiring someone to help him at the shop. I'm glad he finally did. And of course he chose someone so young. He loved being around young people, said it made him feel more like his mischievous self again. I guess he was quite the prankster in his youth."

"I'm not sure he ever outgrew it," Lena said, still tasting a hint of salt on her tongue.

Finally, when Viv had managed to go through a couple of closets and decide which things should be donated or thrown out, she got to her feet. "I think that's enough for today. Let's get you home."

Lena nodded and followed Viv to her car, texting her dad to let him know she was on her way. As she put her bike in the trunk, Lena told Viv about Aunt Teresa's newest side business—doing in-home cat manicures—and about her aunt trying to fix Lena's dad up with people from her book club.

Viv laughed. "Teresa always loved playing matchmaker, especially when we were in college. I probably shouldn't tell her I'm single now or I'll be on her radar again."

When they were almost at Lena's house, Lena got a

message from Marcus: New assignment in five minutes. Make sure to do deep breathing.

She instantly closed her eyes and started imagining herself on a beach, the way her father had instructed, and breathing in and out in a steady rhythm.

"Are you okay?" Viv asked.

"Just feeling a little carsick," she said. Then she went back to concentrating as hard as she could. There was no way she was going to let things get messed up this time.

chapter 18

When Marcus got to Lena's house that night, he was shaking from head to toe. Partly he was nervous about finally meeting Lena's dad, but mostly he was afraid of how Lena would react to his newest assignment.

He glanced at the message on his phone one more time, making triple-sure that he hadn't misread it, but there was no mistaking what it said. Ken Perris, age 38.

Marcus was supposed to zap Lena's dad.

He was so busy planning what he'd say to Lena that he wasn't prepared for Mr. Perris to open the door.

"You must be Marcus!" Mr. Perris said. "Come on in."

Marcus took a deep breath and went over what Grandpa Joe's dating book said about meeting a girl's parents. *Be courteous and trustworthy.* He thought he could manage that, even if the idea of having to zap Mr. Perris in a few minutes was making his stomach churn.

"Lena's running a little late," Mr. Perris said as he waved Marcus inside. "But she should be here soon."

In the living room, Professor was frantically searching for a "gift" to bring him. Finally, the dog appeared with a coaster in his mouth.

"Thanks, Professor," Marcus said, taking the slobbery offering before casually chucking it under the coffee table.

"Do you want something to drink?" Mr. Perris asked.

"No, thank you." He didn't want to risk spilling anything on his neatly ironed shirt. He cleared his throat, trying to remember something from the list of standby pleasantries in Grandpa's book. "You have a nice home here."

"Thank you! Lena did most of the decorating." Mr. Perris motioned to the handmade quilts hanging around the house. "She tells me you restore model spaceships?"

"Yes, sir." He went to explain about the new space shuttle he was working on, but for some reason, he started naming the parts he needed to find. Then he went on to listing types of glue. What was wrong with him? It didn't help that Marcus's cologne was making his eyes itch more than usual, so he kept blinking and blinking like some kind of creepy marionette.

When Mr. Perris got up to feed the dog, Marcus glanced at the time and realized he had five minutes until the match. He quickly sent Lena a message telling her to do her deep breathing. He felt guilty not warning her that her dad was the target of the assignment, but that wasn't the kind of thing he could tell her over a text message. Besides, if she knew the truth, there was no way she could stay calm, no matter how much she was breathing. This way, he might have a chance of doing the assignment right.

"So, Marcus," Mr. Perris said, perching in a nearby armchair again, "do you have any other hobbies, besides your models?"

"Oh, um. Not really, sir. Not besides your daughter!" Too late, he realized that he'd come off sounding like a stalker. Great.

His phone started beeping in his pocket. It was time. He reached out his hand, willing his energy to spark, and hoped that wherever Lena was, she was as calm as could be.

"You're a lifesaver, Lena," Viv said, following her up the walkway. "I've been working on this quilt for ages, and it'll never get done without some help."

"I've got tons of books you can borrow," Lena said. "I'm sure one of them will help you get unstuck."

She opened her front door, took one step inside, and froze as she spotted Marcus in the living room, his hand hovering above her dad's shoulder and glowing bright red.

"What are you doing?" Lena cried.

Marcus stumbled back, his energy fading from his fingers. Did that mean her dad was safe?

"Dad!" Lena said, running up to him. "Are you okay?" But when she looked into his eyes, she knew it was too late. He already had the dazed expression on his face that Lena had seen when she'd foolishly cast a love spell on him a few weeks earlier.

"Hi, Chipmunk," her dad said, staring into space. She was surprised he even knew she was there.

She grabbed Marcus's arm and dragged him into the kitchen. "What...? How...?" She couldn't even find the right question to ask.

"I know it's nuts," Marcus said, "but this is the target Eddie sent me."

"That makes no sense!" Lena cried, finding her voice again. "My dad just had that whole thing with Marguerite, and it was a total disaster. Besides, there's not even anyone here for him to—"

"Hello?" Viv called out from the hallway.

Lena's jaw dropped open. She'd completely forgotten about Viv.

"Hello?" her dad called back. "Is someone here?"

"Dad, no!" Lena cried, running out into the hallway, but it was too late. He and Viv were already standing face-to-face and grinning at each other like lovestruck monkeys.

"Viv, is that you?" her dad asked, gazing at her as if through a fog.

"Ken," she said, "it's so great to see you!"

Lena hurried toward them, yelling, "Sorry, Viv. You have to go home now!"

"Lena, there's nothing you can do," Marcus called after her. "This is what's supposed to happen."

But that couldn't be right. Her dad had said he was interested in dating again, not in falling in love. Not so soon. He wasn't ready. *Lena* wasn't ready!

"Come in, come in." Her dad waved Viv inside, oblivious to the fact that Lena was blocking the doorway.

"Dad!" Lena cried. "Can I talk to you for a minute?"

He gave her a vague wave. "We'll talk later, Chipmunk. We have a guest."

Lena watched, helpless, as he and Viv sauntered into the living room together, practically arm in arm.

"Were you calm before you came through the door?" Marcus whispered in her ear. "Were your emotions under control when I zapped him?"

She realized with horror what he meant. Not only had her dad been matched with someone, but it could be yet another disaster thanks to their malfunctioning powers.

"I don't know," she said. "I was trying to imagine that I was on a beach, but for some reason, I kept picturing Professor's water dish instead."

She turned to look at her dad and Viv again, who were now sitting on the couch in the living room, grinning at each other while they chatted about absolutely nothing. She strained to see sparks around them but only detected a vague yellow aura.

Her dad looked happy. But did he look *too* happy? She couldn't tell. And Viv seemed nice enough, but what if she turned out to be crazy? Thanks to her and Marcus's emotions, anything could happen. And that, Lena realized, was the scariest part.

chapter 19

"Do you want me to ride home with you?" Marcus asked after play rehearsal the next day.

"Did your dating book tell you to offer to do stuff like that?" Lena teased, keeping one eye on the parking lot. She hoped her mom didn't show up until after Marcus was gone.

"Busted," he said. "It's always going on about being a gentleman and 'seeing the lady home safely.' But really, I don't mind."

"That's okay," she said. "I'm, um, going to hang around here and see if I can talk some sense into Hayleigh and Abigail."

"Are you sure? Last I saw, they were fighting over who gets to zip up Emery's backpack for him. It might be a while."

Lena shrugged. "I can wait. You go on ahead."

He shuffled his feet for a second, as if he were looking for the right words. "I'm sorry again," he finally said. "About the whole thing with your dad yesterday."

"Oh, Marcus, I know it's not your fault," she said, trying

to push down the irrational icky feelings that started to swirl inside her whenever she remembered Marcus's glowing hand touching her dad's shoulder. Marcus had only been following orders after all. It made no sense to blame him. And since her dad had a date with Viv that night, Lena would simply have to grin and pretend she was fine with it.

"Okay. I'll talk to you later," Marcus said before finally hopping on his bike and riding away.

Lena sighed in relief as he disappeared down the street. She hadn't told him that her mom was still in town, and if she admitted that the two of them were meeting to talk about Arizona again, she knew he wouldn't take it well. Even though not telling him wasn't lying, not exactly, she still felt bad. But with their powers already on the fritz thanks to their emotions, the less she upset him, the better.

It was freezing out, so Lena wrapped her coat tightly around her, jumping at every car that drove by. If she did wind up going to Arizona, at least the weather would be a little nicer.

What would it be like not to see Marcus every day? Now that he was a part of her life, it felt like he was a puzzle piece she hadn't even realized was missing. Despite all the drama with their powers, Lena couldn't remember ever laughing so much before she'd started spending time with him. Would all that change if she was suddenly living thousands of miles away?

But Natalie was right, Lena reminded herself. If she didn't give her mom a chance, she might regret it. Even if she'd rather be out searching for the soul she'd lost than sitting through a potentially awkward dinner with her mom.

But the truth was Lena didn't know where else to look for Mr. Watts. Even though his pranks were everywhere—this morning she'd woken up with a mustache drawn on her face in red lipstick—she hadn't actually seen the ball of light in a couple of days. Maybe she did need help, but as far as she knew, Eddie still hadn't found a soul hunter to take the job. She had to look harder, that was all.

Suddenly, a wave of giggles erupted behind her. But this time it wasn't Mr. Watts. Lena jumped out of the way as Abigail and Hayleigh practically dragged Emery out of the school.

"How about you come over, and I'll make you cookies?" Hayleigh was asking him.

"Or you could come to my house, and I can bake you a cake," Abigail offered.

"I have a turtle!" Hayleigh cried. "If you want him, you can take him home with you!"

Abigail faltered for a second. "I…I can get my mom to take us shopping and maybe I could convince her to buy you something. What do you want? A shirt? New sneakers? Or do you want money? I can give you my allowance!"

Anna Staniszewski

Meanwhile, Emery was grinning as he looked back and forth between them, as if he didn't realize how scary they were being. "You're great," he was saying. "You're both great."

Oh boy. "Emery," Lena broke in, "I think I saw your mom waiting for you in the back parking lot. You should probably go."

He blinked slowly. "Really? Oh. Okay." He untangled himself from the girls' arms. "Sorry. I guess I should go."

"But you can't!" Hayleigh cried.

"Please!" Abigail said. "Stay with me!"

"You'll see him tomorrow," Lena assured them. "I promise."

They both looked suspicious but finally let go of Emery. He didn't move until Lena gave him a little push toward the parking lot.

"Are you guys okay?" Lena asked when he was gone.

Her friends blinked at her, the hazy looks on their faces slowly fading until they were almost like themselves again.

"Lena, what are you still doing here?" Abigail asked.

"Waiting for my ride," she said, not able to look her in the eye. She knew Abigail would hate that Lena was even considering giving her mom another chance. After all, Abigail had been the one to cheer Lena up on a daily basis after her mom had left in fifth grade.

"Do you want to come with me?" Hayleigh asked. "My dad can drop you off."

126

"That's okay," Lena started to say, but Abigail cut her off.

"Wait," she said to Hayleigh. "I thought you said you had to go straight home. That's why you couldn't give me a ride."

"That's right," Hayleigh shot back. "I couldn't give *you* a ride. Not until you stop trying to take Emery away from me. I've liked him forever!"

Abigail rolled her eyes. "A few weeks isn't forever. Besides, he doesn't even know you exist. I heard him call you 'Hannah' the other day."

"That's because he knows I want to change my name."

"Since when?" Abigail asked with a snort.

"None of your business," Hayleigh said.

"If you say so."

"I *do* say so."

"Fine."

"Fine!"

The two turned up their noses and marched off in opposite directions. Neither of them seemed to remember that Lena was still there.

She glanced at the time and slumped on the stairs. Her mom was supposed to be here any second, but Lena had spent way too many hours waiting to get picked up from school and music lessons and science camp when she was younger to think her mom could ever be punctual. That's why she was shocked when a dark car pulled up less than a minute later and her mom's smiling face peered out the window.

"Hop in!" she said.

Lena glanced around to make sure no one was watching, and then she got in the passenger seat.

"Thank you for meeting me, honey," her mom said. "It means a lot that you'd give me another chance."

Lena swallowed, suddenly feeling bad that she hadn't wanted to, at least not at first. "Where are we going?" she asked, expecting her mom to have already picked a restaurant. Her mom didn't usually like it when other people made decisions for her.

So Lena was surprised yet again when her mom declared, "Your choice!"

Lena studied her out of the corner of her eye as they headed toward her favorite Thai restaurant across town. Her mom looked mostly like herself, though a little more polished than normal, but she wasn't acting like herself at all. Maybe she was only pretending to be a new and improved version of herself, but Lena realized that part of her—a surprisingly big part— hoped that this new Mom was here to stay.

chapter 20

M arcus was about to get ready for bed when Ann-Marie poked her head into his room.

"Dad said to remind you that it's your turn to do the trash this week," she said.

"Okay, thanks," he mumbled, barely looking up as he finished carefully arranging the newly painted shuttle parts by the window to dry.

He expected his sister to duck back out, but instead she said, "What happened to your models? Didn't you have a bunch more of them the other day?"

"Yeah, so?" He straightened up, wiping his hands on his jeans.

"I know you didn't suddenly smarten up and throw them away. Where are they?"

"I...I sold a few of them," he admitted before he pushed past her into the hallway. He knew from experience that it was better to tell his sister the truth rather than have her drag it out of him.

"You *sold* them?" Ann-Marie repeated, following him to the bathroom. She was acting as if he'd told her he'd eaten them with a side of ketchup.

"You were the one talking about throwing them away!"

"I was joking," she said. "I don't know why, but Grandpa loved those dumb things. Remember when he brought you that robot one, and Dad freaked out because he thought you were playing with action figures again?"

Marcus had to chuckle at the memory, even though it wasn't all that funny. "Grandpa swore to me that if Dad kept giving me a hard time, he'd start buying me dolls to mess with him."

Ann-Marie smiled, but he could see her gaze was far away. He and his sister didn't agree on much, but he knew they both missed Grandpa like crazy.

Then her smile disappeared. "If he loved those things so much, how could you get rid of them?"

"Because I need the money," Marcus snapped, hating the accusing tone in her voice. He turned away from her and glopped some toothpaste onto his toothbrush.

"Let me guess, money to impress Lena?" His sister shook her head. "God, Marcus, you're such a people pleaser. You're going to hockey games even though you hate them and bending over backward to make that girlfriend like you. Why can't you let things happen the way they're supposed to?"

Marcus spit into the sink. "Oh, so it's better to be like you? Standing by and hoping something will happen?"

"What's that supposed to mean?"

"Come on, it's obvious you like Peter Chung, but you won't do anything about it. If I wasn't trying to help you, then—"

Ann-Marie's eyes widened in horror. "What are you talking about? What have you been doing?"

"Nothing!" It was technically the truth. At this rate, it didn't seem like fixing up Ann-Marie was ever going to happen.

But his sister clearly didn't believe him. "I don't want you anywhere near Peter again," she said through her teeth. Her jaw was set so tightly, it looked like it might crack. "If I see you even breathing in his direction, I'll tell everyone at your school that you still sleep with your baby blanket. Got it?"

"I don't—" he started to object, but Ann-Marie was already storming down the hall. A second later, her door banged shut.

"Who's slamming doors in this house?" their dad yelled from the kitchen, but he sounded too distracted to come investigate.

With a sigh, Marcus finished brushing his teeth and retreated to his bedroom. He picked up the small pillow that his mom had sewn for him years ago using pieces of his favorite childhood blanket. He didn't actually sleep with it or anything, just kept it on his bed sometimes, but leave it up to Ann-Marie to make the whole thing seem shameful.

He put the pillow aside and changed into his pajamas, his sister's words still bouncing around in his head. He couldn't believe she'd accused him of being a people pleaser when she was the biggest one he'd ever met. Everything she did was designed to make their dad happy.

He climbed into bed as the ghost cat curled up in its favorite spot beside his pillow. Marcus gently stroked its invisible back, feeling a hint of warmth under his fingers. As he glanced at the models around his room, he was surprised that Ann-Marie had even noticed any of them were missing. He'd only sold a few, one to Caspar and a couple to one of the guys in his gym class.

No matter what Ann-Marie thought, selling them hadn't been easy. They were one of his last links to Grandpa Joe after all. But his sister didn't understand. Marcus wasn't the kind of guy who got the girl. Now that he had Lena, he had to do whatever it took to keep her.

chapter 21

Lena was frantically running around the kitchen, trying to shove a banana in her mouth and tie her shoe at the same time, when her dad groggily emerged from his bedroom.

"Chipmunk, what are you doing?" he asked.

"Getting ready for school! I overslept!"

Her dad looked at her as if she'd suddenly started communicating in Morse code. "It's five thirty in the morning."

Lena stopped in her tracks. "What are you talking about?" When her alarm had gone off, it had said she was already late. She'd figured she'd accidentally set it for the wrong time. But now she realized that it was even darker outside than usual, and the entire neighborhood was quiet and still. Ugh! This had to be another one of Mr. Watts's jokes!

"Sorry to wake you," she told her dad, still trying to catch her breath. "I guess I'm kind of confused this morning."

He gave her a drowsy smile and headed back to his room. Lena realized as she closed the door that she'd forgotten to ask him about his date with Viv the previous night. She seriously hoped they hadn't gotten matching tattoos or something.

She was too wired to go back to bed, so Lena decided to work on her mom's quilt for a while. At this rate, she'd have it done well before Christmas. As she worked, she tried to come up with her next step for tracking down Mr. Watts's soul. She'd thought she could check out where he'd gone to school, but when she'd looked it up online, she'd discovered that his elementary and high schools had long since been bulldozed to make room for a strip mall. Viv had said Mr. Watts didn't have any family, but maybe there was some long-lost relative Lena could track down. She didn't know what else to do.

Two hours later, when it was actually time to leave for school, Lena's phone rang. She smiled when she saw it was her mom calling. They'd had a surprisingly nice time at dinner the night before. Her mom hadn't pressured her about Arizona at all, only told her about some of the fun things they might do together. The more they'd talked about it, the more Lena had started to warm up to the idea. But when she thought about uprooting her life, even for a little while, her chest still tightened. It felt like such a big step.

"I know we don't have plans until tonight," her mom said, "but I'm outside your door. I was thinking I could give you a ride to school. And how about you bring Professor with you, and I'll take him to the park and drop him off tonight."

"I'll be right out," Lena said, grinning despite herself. She could imagine Abigail accusing her of being won over too easily, but she couldn't help it. Her mom did seem different.

She put Professor on a leash and headed out to her mom's car. When she opened the back door, Professor hopped onto the seat, wagging his tail in excitement as he licked her mom's face.

"I miss having a pet," her mom said, giggling as he started nibbling on her hair. "Did you eat breakfast? We could stop somewhere on the way."

"That sounds good," Lena said, realizing that she hadn't eaten since her early morning banana.

As they pulled out of the driveway, Lena had a sudden feeling of déjà vu. This was what things used to be like before her mom left. She couldn't deny that she'd missed it, no matter how much she hadn't wanted to admit it to herself.

"Mom, I was thinking about what we could do tonight. There's a new fabric store that opened up near the movie theater. Maybe we could check it out."

A pained look flashed across her mom's face, and Lena's feeling of déjà vu came on even stronger. It was the look her mom had given her dozens of times when she'd had to cancel plans at the last second or skip Lena's science fair or school concert because she had to work. She knew the words that came next all too well.

"I wish I could, but—" her mom began.

"That's okay," Lena cut her off. "I have homework I have to do tonight anyway."

Her mom made a strange choking sound and said, "No, it's not okay."

She abruptly pulled the car over onto the side of the road. A truck behind them honked in annoyance, but her mom didn't seem to notice.

Meanwhile, Professor tried to jump into the front seat, only managing to wedge his German shepherd head and oversized paws into Lena's lap.

"Mom, what are we doing?" she asked through a mouthful of fur. "Why did you stop?"

"Because I need to tell you something." She took in a long breath, as if she were about to break some bad news. "The reason I can't meet you tonight is because I'll be out tracking down a soul."

Lena blinked, sure she'd heard wrong. "A what?"

"A soul. The one that got away from you, in fact. I don't normally work in this territory, but when Eddie called me—"

"Wait, Eddie? My boss Eddie?" This didn't make sense.

None of this made sense. Lena's mom was talking about souls as if they…as if she… "You're a—?"

"Yes, honey. I'm a soul hunter, or at least I'm training to be one. I haven't been officially promoted yet, so for now, I'm still a soul collector like you are."

Lena felt her eyes bulge out of her head. "What?" she whispered. "Since when are you a… That's impossible. You're…"

"I've been trying to think of the best way to tell you, and finally I decided there was no good way. I just needed to do it."

"That's impossible!" Lena said again. And this time she was shouting. Her mom wasn't a soul *anything*. She was a nurse!

Her mom smiled sadly. "I know it's a lot to take in. If you want, I can write you a note so you can skip your morning classes, and we can go talk about all of this over bagels."

"Bagels?" Lena erupted, making Professor whimper in her lap. "I haven't seen you in almost a year, and then you show up and say you want me to come live with you. And now, as if that wasn't crazy enough, you announce you're training to be a soul hunter, and you want us to go eat breakfast and act like everything is fine?"

"Lena—"

She couldn't breathe, and it wasn't only the fact that Professor was crushing her. The car suddenly felt small and airless, like a metal coffin. Lena threw open the car door and tumbled out.

"Wait!" her mom cried. "We're not done talking!"

Professor barked woefully as if he agreed. But Lena had never felt so done in her entire life.

When she got to school, Lena was dripping with sweat. She'd hoped if she ran as fast as possible, she could get ahead of everything that had just happened. If the whole acting thing didn't work out, maybe she should try out for the track team next year, she thought wildly.

She was gasping for air when she got to Marcus's locker.

"Are you okay?" he asked. "What happened?"

"Come on," she said, dragging him to the auditorium. She was still having trouble catching her breath, but once they'd sunk into a couple of seats, Lena managed to cough out the gist of what had happened. Marcus's eyes grew wider with every word.

"So your mom is—"

"Training to be a soul hunter. A *soul hunter*! Can you believe it?"

He shook his head. "That's nuts. But…in a way, it makes sense that she's a soul collector, doesn't it? I mean, you said she was always working when she still lived with you. She was probably spending all that time doing assignments."

Lena stared at him. It hadn't occurred to her that her mom wasn't only a soul collector now but that she'd been one for years.

"How could she lie to me like that? And Eddie knew what she was and didn't say anything." She jumped to her feet and started pacing up and down the aisle. "I can't believe this! For all I know, she's been lying to me for my whole life!"

"But you know she couldn't tell you. You haven't told your dad about your powers, have you?"

"That's different! I'm her daughter! And now she shows up and drops this bomb on me as if it's no big deal. As if it doesn't totally affect my decision to go live with her!"

She realized the instant the words were out of her mouth that she'd made a huge mistake.

Marcus's eyes grew wider and wider. "Wait. What do you mean you're going to live with her?"

Lena sighed, knowing she had to tell him the whole truth now. "I was thinking about it, but obviously that's not going to happen."

"So you were planning on leaving, and you didn't tell me?"

"I know I should have, but…at first, I wasn't even considering it. Then Natalie started talking about how much she regretted not getting to know her dad, which got me thinking about stuff with my mom. She also said I shouldn't say anything to you about moving, since it would only make you upset. And she was right, wasn't she? If I'd told you and then you'd gone on an assignment, it would have made our powers go crazy again. Besides, it doesn't matter anymore, because I'm not going anywhere with my mother."

But she could tell by the look on his face that it did matter. The bell for homeroom rang, and he got to his feet. "I have to go."

"Marcus, I'm sorry—"

"I'll see you later," he said flatly. Then he turned and left the auditorium, the door swinging shut behind him with an echoing thud.

chapter 22

Marcus's whole body felt numb as he stumbled toward his locker. Lena had been planning to move, and she'd hidden it from him? He'd thought they were perfect for each other and that she was the closest person to him in his life now that Grandpa was gone. Clearly, she didn't feel that way about him. Is this what Eddie had meant when he'd said that Marcus and Lena were on different frequencies? And Marcus had stupidly objected, claiming everything between them was perfect.

As he rounded the corner, he spotted Emery standing in the middle of the hallway with Abigail on one side and Hayleigh on the other. Marcus kept hoping that the sparks between them would fade, but so far they were bouncing around, wild as ever. He shook his head in disgust and started to stomp away, but then he noticed what looked like an enormous pile of meat at Hayleigh's side. As if that weren't strange enough, the meat appeared to be on wheels.

Curious, Marcus drew closer and heard Hayleigh saying,

"I noticed you eat the same thing for lunch almost every day, so...ta-da! I made a sculpture of you out of meat loaf!"

Sure enough, when Marcus looked carefully, he could see something that almost looked like Emery's profile carved into the meaty mound. Gross.

"What do you want him to do with that? Eat it?" Abigail shot back. "I gave him a way better present." She flashed Emery a sweet smile. "It was delivered last night. Right, Emery?"

Emery nodded. "My dad had to help me bring it upstairs. It takes up most of my room."

Abigail beamed in triumph. "I knew you'd like it!" She turned to Hayleigh. "I had a portrait made of him that's larger than life-size. That means Emery can hang a picture of himself on the wall that's bigger than he is!"

"Which one do you like more?" Hayleigh asked.

"Yeah, Emery," Abigail chimed in. "Which one is better?"

There was something in both of their eyes that made Marcus think of starved animals. He couldn't watch this anymore. He swooped in, grabbed Emery, and dragged him toward the bathroom despite Hayleigh and Abigail's objections.

When they were alone, Emery's mind seemed to clear a little. "Oh, hey, Marcus," he said. "What's up?"

"Are you okay?" Marcus asked. "It looked like those girls were about to tear you apart."

Emery shrugged, glancing at himself in the bathroom mirror. "I...I don't know. I'm so confused. They want me to choose between them, but I don't want to choose. But maybe I should choose. But what if I hurt their feelings? I mean, I do like them, I guess. But what if I don't? You know?"

"Keep avoiding them for as long as you can," Marcus said, wishing he could do more to help. "It'll all work itself out." At least, he hoped so. The truth was, after what had happened with Lena, he wasn't sure he had much hope left.

As if Marcus being mad at her wasn't bad enough, Lena found a furious-looking Abigail waiting for her at her locker after third period.

"Why didn't you tell me your mom was in town?" she demanded. For once, she looked like her normal non-love-crazed self, and her normal self was clearly hurt. Lena almost wished Emery would walk by and distract her.

"Who said she was in town?" Lena asked slowly.

"I saw you getting in a car with her last night. Why didn't you say anything?"

There was no point in hiding the truth anymore, especially now that Marcus knew everything. "Because I didn't want you to judge me, okay?" Lena said. "If I told you that she'd come back into town and asked me to live with her, I knew you'd bring up how much she hurt me when we were younger."

"Why would I judge you?" Abigail asked. "If you want to give your mom another chance, that's your business. I'd want you to be careful, but I'd also want you to do whatever made you happy."

Lena blinked. "Really?"

"Duh! I'm your friend, remember?" She shook her head. "But I don't get why you'd lie to me. Not only about that but also about Natalie."

"When did I lie about Natalie?"

"You said your dad worked with her dad, but when I asked her about it, she had no idea what I was talking about. Why would you make something like that up?"

Lena had no answer to that. What could she say that wasn't yet another lie?

"You're not even going to try to explain?" Abigail asked in disbelief. "I thought we were best friends!"

"We are!"

"I don't think so," Abigail said. "Best friends trust each other. They tell each other stuff. It's felt like you've been hiding things from me for months. If you don't trust me—"

"I *do* trust you!" Lena cried.

"I don't think you trust anyone but yourself," Abigail shot

back. Then she stormed down the hall to where Hayleigh was waiting for her. The two of them gave Lena a collective glare and walked away. Apparently, being mad at her was the one thing her friends could agree on.

chapter 23

Marcus was pretending to paint yet another tree in the back of the auditorium as he watched Lena out of the corner of his eye. She was waiting on the edge of the stage for her turn to act as if her character lived on Mars. He could see the skeptical look on her face, and he could practically hear her thinking that the exercise was a waste of time. That's how well he knew her, and yet he felt like there was a big part of her he didn't understand. How could she be so furious with her mom for keeping things from her and then turn around and do the exact same thing to Marcus?

"Watch out," Hayleigh said beside him. Marcus realized he'd dripped green paint on the floor. He quickly wiped it off and tried to focus on his work again, but his eyes kept wandering back to the stage.

Mr. Jackson clapped his hands and told everyone to team up to do trust falls—another activity he could tell Lena hated. He expected her to pair up with Abigail, but instead Lena asked Connie Reynolds to be her partner.

As they went in the corner, Connie whispered something to Lena, and then the two of them looked out at Marcus and giggled. Were they really laughing at him in front of his face?

He splattered more green on the floor, but he didn't care. Instead, he kept attacking the tree with his brush, imagining what he would tell Grandpa if he were here. "I thought I'd gotten the girl, but it turned out she was planning to move and didn't tell me."

Suddenly, someone onstage screamed. Marcus's eyes snapped up. Connie was sprawled on the stage, cradling her left wrist in her right hand.

"Ow, it hurts! It hurts!" she cried. "I think it's broken!"

Mr. Jackson ran over as Abigail helped Connie to her feet. "What happened?" he yelled.

"Lena dropped me!" Connie said, bursting into tears.

"I…I'm sorry," Lena said, her face nearly white. "I tried to catch her, but…"

"All right," Mr. Jackson said when she didn't go on. "We'll talk in a minute. Abigail and Hayleigh, bring Connie to the nurse's office. Everyone else, go home. Rehearsal is over."

The cast and crew left the auditorium in silence. Marcus dragged his feet as much as he could, so that he was still in the room when he heard Mr. Jackson say, "I'm sorry, Lena. I thought when I cast you that you were a team player, but—" Then he spotted Marcus and yelled, "I said, get out!"

Marcus had no choice but to do just that.

Lena heard the words coming out of Mr. Jackson's mouth, but she couldn't believe they were real. Mr. Jackson couldn't be kicking her out of the play.

"But I did all those weird character exercises," she said weakly. "And my dad's almost finished making my costume. It looks all wrong, but he worked hard on it. And…and…" How could she explain to him that he was crushing her dreams? And how could she convince him that she'd only dropped Connie because she'd been trying to protect her?

"I'm sorry," Mr. Jackson said. "When you missed rehearsal the other day, I was concerned. And after what just happened, I think this is what's best for everyone. I thought that if you spent enough time with the cast, you'd start to learn to trust the process. But—"

"I do trust the process!" Lena cried. "I did everything you told us to do!"

"You did it, but you didn't really believe it." He got to his feet. "I have to go check on Connie. If you want to try out for the high school play next year, that's fine, but let's let this one go, okay?"

Then he left her alone in the empty auditorium. She sat there, not moving, for what felt like an hour. Finally, the door creaked open, and Marcus tiptoed in.

"Are you okay?" he whispered, sitting down beside her.

"My fingers started glowing."

"What?"

"I was about to catch Connie, like I was supposed to, and then my fingers started glowing for no reason. Mr. Jackson doesn't understand. I *couldn't* catch her. If I had, she'd be dead!"

Marcus stared at her. "But why would your fingers be glowing like that?" And then he seemed to understand. "My emotions did that?"

"And now I'm not in the play anymore."

"He really kicked you out?" Marcus asked, his eyes widening. "But the play is in a week! What are they going to do?"

"I only have one line. Anyone can replace me." Lena had convinced herself that her part was important, that she had to take it as seriously as if she were the lead. But the truth was, Mr. Jackson had probably already given someone else the part. "Why would you do that to me, Marcus?"

"What are you talking about?"

How could he not get it? "Whatever you were feeling, it got me kicked out of the play!"

"You're the one who lied to me! And then you and Connie were laughing at me in front of my face. How do you want me to feel?" He was panting now, as if he'd run one of his sister's track races.

"We weren't laughing at you," Lena said. "Connie was saying how cute you were and how lucky I am to—" But Marcus didn't give her a chance to finish.

"The worst part is you're so mad at your mom, but you can't see that you're exactly like her!"

"What's that supposed to mean?" Lena started to ask, but then her fingers were suddenly glowing again. "Stop it!" she cried, jumping back in her seat to be as far away from Marcus as possible. One touch and she could kill him.

"I'm not doing anything," he said as his hand flared to life too. He got to his feet, staring at his red fingers. "I should go. It's too dangerous for us to be in the same room right now."

"Marcus, wait!" She couldn't let him leave like this, not when they were both so mad. But he was already gone.

chapter 24

As Marcus hurried away from the auditorium—and away from Lena—his hand gradually stopped glowing. He got to the lobby and sucked in a few breaths until the suffocating feeling in his chest finally faded.

At the bottom of the school's front steps, he spotted Natalie waiting on a bench. Suddenly, he remembered what Eddie had said during his test of their powers. "Lena told Natalie that she doesn't really like you." The anger that was already brewing inside him flared in his chest at the sight of her.

"You!" he said, marching up to her. "What have you been saying to Lena?"

Her pale eyebrows scrunched in confusion. "What are you talking about? I've been trying to help."

"Help with what?"

Natalie didn't answer. Her eyes suddenly glazed over, and she stared straight ahead with a strange, vacant expression.

"Are you okay?" Marcus asked, but she didn't move. He

waved his hand in front of her face, but she only kept staring straight ahead. What was going on?

Then, as suddenly as it had come, the episode passed. Natalie sucked in a breath like she'd emerged from a long underwater dive.

"What happened?" Marcus asked, but Natalie wasn't listening. She grabbed her green notebook from her pocket and started scribbling furiously. "Natalie, talk to me! Is everything all right?"

When she still didn't respond, he snatched the notebook away from her. She shrieked as if he'd physically hurt her. "Give that back!"

"What are you always writing in here?" he asked, glancing at the open page. He only saw a few words, but they were enough to make his breath stop in his chest.

Lena and Marcus apart. Alice ruined by red.

"Why are you writing stuff about us?" Marcus flipped back and saw there were pages of scribbles, some so cramped that they were totally illegible. "What is all this?"

Natalie let out a defeated sigh. "It's the future."

"Is that supposed to explain things? What do you mean it's the future?"

She snatched her notebook back and stuffed it in her pocket. "Forget it," she said, but Marcus wasn't going to let her go, not when he'd finally started to get something like the truth from her.

"Natalie, please," he said, jumping in front of her. "If you know something, tell me. What do you mean it's the future? Is the stuff in your notebook…?" He gasped. "Is it stuff that hasn't happened yet?"

She rolled her eyes. "That's kind of the definition of the future, isn't it?"

"But how?"

She glanced around as if making sure they were alone. "You're a matchmaker," she said softly. "Well, I'm a seer. Like an oracle but without all that speaking in tongues and wearing ugly robes nonsense."

Marcus probably shouldn't have been surprised. If he could match people and Lena could guide souls into the afterlife, why couldn't there be people who saw the future? But it seemed impossible! "I thought you were a soul collector like Lena."

"What?" Natalie asked, looking momentarily confused. "Oh, yeah, I'm both." She shrugged. "It's rare to have more than one ability, I guess, but it happens."

"So when you freeze like that, you see what's going to happen?"

She nodded. "Most of the time I'm only out for a minute, but sometimes it's like I'm sleepwalking. I'll wake up and not know how I got somewhere. Or I don't remember being there at all. Like the hockey game."

"So you *were* there!"

"I guess. If you hadn't asked me about it, I wouldn't have known, although I could tell I had a vision that day because there was new stuff written in my notebook. It's..." She looked at her feet. "It's kind of scary not remembering part of your day, but it comes with the territory."

"And just now you saw that the play was going to get 'ruined by red' and that Lena and I are going to break up?" Yesterday, he would have said that was insane, but after everything that had happened between them today, maybe his relationship wasn't as solid as he'd thought. But that future couldn't happen. Lena was his match. Even if things were rough right now, he couldn't imagine life without her.

"Half the time I don't even know what the stuff I write down means," Natalie said, but he could tell she was only saying that to make him feel better.

"But the future isn't fixed, right?" Marcus asked, thinking back to all the time travel movies he'd seen. "We can keep it from happening, can't we?"

Natalie only gave him a pitying look and said, "I'm sorry, Marcus. The future is meant to happen for a reason. There's nothing you can do."

chapter 25

When her dad came home from work that night, Lena was curled up on the couch, watching out the window as the squirrel busied herself gathering seeds that Lena had sprinkled for her. She wondered if the squirrel missed Professor when he wasn't there, or if she only remembered that she had a dog husband when he was right in front of her face.

"What's wrong, Chipmunk?" her dad asked.

"It was a long day."

That, at least, was the truth. She couldn't believe everything that had happened in the span of twenty-four hours. Was her dad the only person who was still even speaking to her?

"The good news is you don't have to worry about finishing that costume," she added. Then she burst into tears.

Her dad rushed over, clearly panicked at the rare sight of her crying. "What happened?" he asked, hugging her tight.

She tried to explain to him about Connie breaking her wrist, but there was so much of the story that she couldn't tell him.

The bottom line was the same though. She was out of the play, and there was nothing she could do to change that.

When the tears finally stopped flowing, Lena felt exhausted but a little lighter. "I'm okay now," she said.

"You know what will make you feel better?" Her dad ruffled the top of her hair. "Physical activity. Come help me make dinner. It'll release some endorphins and improve your mood."

Lena got to her feet and followed him into the kitchen, her body moving like it was on autopilot. As she started peeling potatoes, her mind was still churning. "Dad, when Mom was still around, did she ever do anything besides her job?" She couldn't imagine how her mom had kept her soul collecting secret from her dad for so long without him getting suspicious.

He thought for a minute. "Her nursing job kept her pretty busy. That's one reason she stopped doing community theater. But she was part of a quilting club at the library that met on the weekends and sometimes in the evenings. They seemed to have a pretty erratic schedule."

Lena nodded to herself. The quilting club must have been her mom's cover for when she'd had to go on assignments. When she'd had to go collect souls.

How could her mom have had a secret identity without Lena knowing? Granted, as far as Lena could tell, her dad had no idea about *her* secret life either. Would he feel as betrayed as she did if he suddenly found out about it? No, she couldn't think about that, not on top of everything else.

When she went to throw away the potato peels, she found her dad's dating chart in the recycling bin. "Um, Dad?" she said. "Does this mean you and Viv had a good date last night?"

A goofy grin spread across her dad's face. "It was great! In some ways, she's exactly how I remember her, but she's much less serious these days. She quit her job as a lawyer and is trying out a career in comedy writing. It's a huge risk, but it seems to be paying off so far. She says she was inspired by her mentor, Watts. And she said you knew him?"

Lena coughed. "Oh, sort of. I went to his shop a couple of times." That wasn't exactly a lie, but she quickly changed the subject. "I bet Aunt Teresa's thrilled about you and Viv."

Her dad laughed. "She claims she always knew we'd make a good couple."

Lena realized that her dad hadn't seemed this happy—genuinely happy—in a long time. Maybe they *were* a good match.

"Do you think you could marry Viv someday?" If this was supposed to be his love match, maybe it was better if Lena was prepared.

"Oh, Chipmunk," he said. "She's not going to replace your mom. You never have to worry about that."

"I know, Dad. That's not what—"

She was interrupted by the doorbell. Her dad went to answer it, whistling happily to himself. If it was Viv, not able to keep herself away because of the love voodoo flowing through her veins, Lena was going to have to hide in her room for the rest of the night.

But it wasn't Viv.

"Jessica!" she heard her dad say. "Lena didn't tell me you were still in town!"

Lena swallowed. She'd been trying to think of a way to tell her dad about Arizona, but nothing had seemed right. She really hoped her mom didn't bring it up now, especially since it didn't matter anyway. There was no way Lena was going to give her mom another chance.

"Come on in!" her dad added. It was strange to hear him being so cheerful around her mom. Usually when Lena's mom came to visit around the holidays, her dad was all business with a hint of sadness underneath. Maybe now that he had Viv, he didn't care about the past as much.

"I'm returning the dog," her mom said. "We had a great time at the park, and Professor was completely ignoring the squirrels! He wouldn't even look at them. I guess you finally trained him to leave them alone." She laughed lightly. "Is Lena home? I was thinking I might take her out for some ice cream."

Lena hovered uncertainly by the microwave. Was food her

mom's solution to everything? She didn't want to see her mom, but she also couldn't ignore her forever. Finally, Lena took a deep breath and went out to face her.

"I'll leave you two alone," her dad said as if he could sense the tension between them. Then he scurried into the living room.

Lena stood and waited for her mom to talk. She definitely wasn't going to be the first one to say anything. Besides, she didn't know what to say.

She expected her mom to start trying to explain again or to apologize, but instead she said in a low voice, "Do you want another shot at catching that lost soul?"

"Absolutely," Lena couldn't help saying. She'd spent a good ten minutes locked in the bathroom this afternoon because Watts had decided it would be hilarious to jam the lock with actual jam. Strawberry. She didn't know how many more of his pranks she could take.

"Good," her mom said. "Then grab your jacket and let's go."

After fifteen minutes in the car with her mom, Lena couldn't stand the silence anymore.

"Where are we going?" she asked when they turned onto the highway. She'd assured her dad that their "ice cream date" wouldn't keep her out too late.

Anna Staniszewski

"Eddie said you tried Watts's store and apartment but that his soul got away," her mom said, her eyes on the road. "That probably means his soul is drawn more strongly to a different place. If you catch him there, he's less likely to run off. I figure we'll try the house where he grew up."

"But Viv told me that he left home when he was still in high school. Would his soul really go back there?"

"You never know where people feel safest." She adjusted the rearview mirror. "Who's Viv?"

Lena hesitated. She couldn't get the words "Dad's new girlfriend" out of her mouth, so instead she said, "One of his comedy students."

"That's right. Eddie told me he used to do stand-up. If his childhood home doesn't work out, we can try some of the clubs where he performed."

Lena couldn't help cringing at the word "we." She wasn't sure she wanted anything to do with her mom right now, but she also couldn't help marveling at how much she was already learning from her about tracking down souls.

When they got to the tiny house where Watts grew up, Lena knew right away that his soul wasn't here. It was the most cheerless place she'd ever seen. The walls were sagging, the shutters were barely hanging on, and the roof looked like it might cave in at any second. There was a faded "For Sale" sign

162

out front, as if someone had put the house on the market years ago and then forgotten all about it.

Lena and her mom peered in through the windows for a few minutes, but the place was obviously deserted. Even though it looked like a haunted house, there were no ghosts here.

"Doesn't smell like popcorn," her mom finally said before heading back to the car.

"Popcorn?" Lena echoed, even though she was still trying to give her mom the cold shoulder.

"I know how it sounds, but I've found that when I'm track-ing a runaway soul, if I smell buttered popcorn, that usually means I'm near the soul's happy place." She laughed. "That's what I call the spot where the soul is at its most comfortable."

Lena didn't answer. It sounded beyond strange, almost like the kind of thing her mom would make up to try to make her smile. But Lena wasn't going to give her the satisfaction.

"So tell me about this boyfriend of yours," her mom said after they'd gotten back in the car.

"Nothing to tell," Lena said. That was one topic she defi-nitely didn't want to discuss, especially with her mom. "Why did you come into town now anyway?" she asked instead. "Why not wait until Christmas?"

"I wasn't planning on being here, but then I talked to Eddie last week for the first time in years, and he told me about you.

I couldn't believe it. My little Lena had become a soul collector just like me! I had to come see it for myself."

"So the only reason you came back was because you found out I'm like you? Otherwise, you wouldn't have cared about seeing me?"

"Of course not!" her mom said. "I think about you all the time, Lena. Even if I'm not here, that doesn't mean—"

But Lena didn't want to hear it. She wanted the truth. "How could you not tell me that you were a soul collector? I can understand keeping it from Dad. He wouldn't understand about souls and stuff. But me?"

"Do you really think you would have understood? You were always my little girl, but in some ways you're very much like your father, only accepting things that you can see with your own eyes."

Lena started to object, but she had to admit her mom was right. If she hadn't spent the past few months collecting souls, she would have never believed such a thing was possible. Even with all of that, she still hadn't wanted to believe that match-makers existed. It was only after she'd had Marcus's powers for a few days that she had finally accepted his job as a real thing.

"So when did you become a soul collector?" Lena asked.

Her mom sighed, like it took effort to think back that far. "I was in college studying to be a nurse, and the two jobs seemed to go together. I could help those who were sick, and when they were dying, I could help them by easing their souls into the After. I met Eddie on one of the first collections I ever did. He was a new matchmaker and also learning the ropes, so we became friends."

"You've known Eddie since college? Why didn't he tell me you were friends?"

"He and I haven't spoken in years. I wasn't even sure we *were* friends anymore, after everything that happened."

"What do you mean?"

But her mom shook her head. "It's not worth getting into now. The important thing is I'm here, and I want us to get to know each other again. You don't know how I felt when I found out that you'd become a soul collector, Lena. I was so proud of you! But I was also worried."

"Worried? Why?"

"Because it's a difficult job. Seeing death all the time, having to take the souls of people you know, people you care about, it wears on you."

"Is that why you left?"

Her mom sighed as she adjusted her rearview mirror for probably the third time. "It took me a long time to accept that being a soul collector was part of my life. I let it ruin so many things: my family, my career. After a while, I couldn't stay here anymore."

Lena picked at some lint on her shirt, thinking about how her own life felt like it was in ruins right now. "And did you finally find a place where you could be happy?"

"I don't know," her mom admitted. "Becoming a soul hunter is something I've wanted for a long time, and I finally found a nursing job I like. But I realized that I could never be happy without you in my life. That's why I want you to come live with me. Think about how much I can teach you!"

For a minute, Lena could almost see it, what life would be like with her mom. They'd be living together in her mom's sunny apartment in Arizona, sharing what they knew about the ins and outs of soul collecting, making quilts together and seeing plays, and maybe even sharing each other's clothes like Abigail and her mom did. It would be almost like the life Lena could have had if her mom hadn't left. And best of all, Lena could finally live in a house where there weren't any secrets.

Maybe that future really could happen—and maybe some part of Lena even wanted it to—but it would mean leaving everything else she cared about behind.

chapter 26

Marcus hovered outside the indoor track after school on Monday, trying to spot Peter without his sister seeing him. Maybe he *was* butting in like she'd said, but he was doing it for her. Once she and Peter were together, she'd thank him.

Finally, he spotted Peter talking to one of the coaches. Thankfully, Claire was nowhere in sight. Good! Maybe the sparks between them were finally starting to fade. Marcus never thought he'd be rooting for one of his matches to fail, but he didn't want a couple to be miserable together just so his perfect matchmaking record could stay intact.

He waited until Peter was alone, and then he made his move. "Hey, how's it going?"

"Hey, Marcus. I saw your sister's race earlier. She was amazing."

"Yeah, she's pretty great." Ann-Marie drove him nuts, but she was definitely incredible when it came to running. Marcus knew he should jump into the script he'd practiced over the weekend—"Will you be going to the play on Friday? My sister wants to go but needs a ride. Maybe the two of you could carpool."—but instead he said, "You can tell that she spends all her time training."

"She does?" Peter asked. "How does she find time to study? I'm in a couple of her classes, and she always aces every test."

"That's, like, her whole life. She doesn't do anything else." Marcus realized that he'd probably made his sister sound like a complete loser. "Not that she doesn't go out with people. She does. She hangs out with her friends and boyfriends and stuff."

"She has a boyfriend?" Peter asked, the disappointment clear in his voice.

"What? Oh, I didn't mean boyfriends. I meant guy friends. She's never actually dated anyone. At least not that she's told me about. I didn't even know she was interested in anyone until I saw how she acted around you." Oh no. Had he really just said that?

Peter's eyebrows shot up. "Wait, do you mean that she's into me?"

"No! Of course not!"

"Oh." Peter's face fell. "Okay. I thought maybe—"

"Cinnamon Knees!" someone called from across the lobby. Of course, it was Claire. "Are you coming? I miss you!"

"I'll be right there!" he called back. Then he turned to Marcus. "Sorry, we have to go to the mall. Claire needs new shoes."

"Um, do you actually want to go buy her shoes?" Marcus couldn't help asking. That didn't sound like fun at all.

Peter frowned. "I...I don't know," he said. "I want to be with her, no matter where we are. Even if that means shopping instead of watching hockey."

This was yet another reason that Ann-Marie and Peter were perfect for each other. She'd choose sports over clothes any day.

"Wait, I wanted to talk to you about the play!" Marcus called, but Peter had already disappeared out the door with Claire, leaving behind a trail of listless sparks.

"Lena, wait up!" Natalie called down the hallway. Lena stopped in front of the library and waited for Natalie to catch up. "I heard about the play. Are you okay?"

"I'm fine," Lena said. The truth was she'd spent all weekend moping around, barely talking to anyone. She dreaded the final bell when all the other kids in the play would go to rehearsal, and she'd head home by herself.

"What about your part?" Natalie asked.

"Mr. Jackson asked Connie Reynolds to do it, since she had

a nonspeaking role before." Lena had apologized profusely to Connie for dropping her. Luckily, Connie hadn't seemed all that bothered by the purple cast on her wrist, since it made people fawn all over her even more than they normally did.

"Wow, I guess Connie is getting all of your leftovers, huh?" Natalie asked.

"What do you mean?"

Natalie gave her a pitying look. "I supposed it's better you hear it from me first. I saw Connie and Marcus flirting in homeroom this morning."

Lena stared. That couldn't be right. "He was probably helping her because she's injured. He's nice like that." Marcus didn't even know how to flirt!

Natalie gave her an "if you say so" look and added, "They were talking about going to see *A Midsummer Night's Dream* together."

"What?" Okay, Lena and Marcus might have had a fight and not spoken for a couple of days, but they hadn't broken up or anything. And now he was going to see the play with Connie when he hadn't wanted to go with her? That was impossible!

Or maybe it wasn't. Lena suddenly remembered what Connie had said about how cute Marcus was, and Lena had stupidly told him about it. Maybe he was sick of dealing with their up-and-down relationship—especially after they'd started accidentally firing their powers at each other!—and he'd decided to go for a nice, regular girl who couldn't kill him with a single touch.

"And there's something else," Natalie said, not looking up from the floor. "I probably should have told you this sooner, but I didn't want to hurt your feelings."

"Tell me," Lena said. "I can handle it."

Natalie bit her lip. "It wasn't just Connie that I saw Marcus flirting with. Last week at lunch, when you left because your mom was here…he was hitting on me too."

Lena opened her mouth, but only air came out.

"I thought maybe I was reading into things," Natalie rushed on. "Or that he was only being friendly. But when I thought about it later…" She shook her head. "I'm sorry."

Lena could barely see straight. What Natalie was saying couldn't be true. But if Marcus could go around making eyes at Connie, why couldn't he flirt with the new girl too? Suddenly, Lena remembered the mysterious exchange she'd seen between Marcus and Caspar in the hallway the other day. Marcus had gotten mad at her for keeping things from him, but he clearly had secrets of his own.

Lena had thought she knew Marcus and that she could trust him, but maybe Eddie was right. Maybe the two of them weren't on the same frequency after all.

Lena wasn't at lunch, and Marcus had only managed to see her from a distance all day, almost as if she'd been avoiding him. It hadn't helped that Connie Reynolds had suddenly decided he was her personal servant because he'd happened to open a door for her that morning. He'd spent the day so far following her around like a pack mule, lugging her enormous bag.

Marcus sat at the lunch table alone, watching across the cafeteria as Abigail and Hayleigh tried to woo Emery with food. Abigail was cutting his meat loaf into tiny pieces and feeding them to him while Hayleigh was shoving carrot sticks into his mouth. Marcus shook his head and mentally reviewed the Heimlich maneuver just in case. Who knew love jolts could be so potentially hazardous to your health?

"Have you seen Lena?" he asked Natalie when she slid her tray on the table. "I need to apologize to her." He'd almost called her several times over the weekend but decided to wait and do it in person. Grandpa's dating book advised always having "heartfelt discussions" face-to-face.

"She's probably home packing," Natalie said, plopping down in a seat across from him.

"Packing?" he repeated. "For what?"

"She didn't tell you? She and her mom patched things up, and she's planning to leave this weekend."

Marcus's sandwich fell out of his hand. "Leave for Arizona? But she said she wasn't going to go anywhere with her mom!"

Natalie shrugged. "I guess she changed her mind."

"But what about the play?"

"She's not in it anymore, remember? She said there was no point in sticking around now that Mr. Jackson kicked her out."

Marcus couldn't believe it. Wasn't *he* a reason to stick around? Even if Lena was still mad at him, wouldn't she at least try to make things right between them before she left?

He pushed his lunch away, his appetite gone. "So is this the future you saw?" Marcus asked. "Lena and I are apart because she dumps me and moves to Arizona?"

Natalie's face softened. "I'm sorry, Marcus. For what it's worth, I think you guys make a great couple. But maybe it's not meant to work out."

Marcus's whole body felt heavy. He'd thought he and Lena were the perfect match, but clearly things had been off between them for a while—whether he realized it or not—for their powers to get so messed up. He couldn't help wondering if the fact that things had been so hard for them from the beginning was a sign.

Then he remembered what Grandpa Joe had always said

about relationships: "They are hard work. If you're coasting, you're doing it wrong."

Maybe he *was* doing it wrong, but he wasn't ready to give up yet.

chapter 27

L ena sat back in her chair, staring at the finished quilt. After weeks of work, it was finally done, and it was the best one she'd ever made. She knew her mom would be proud of her when she saw it.

The doorbell rang, and she hid the quilt in her closet, just in case it was her mom. Lena certainly didn't want to spoil the Christmas surprise. But when Lena opened the front door, she found Marcus staring back at her.

"Stay back!" she cried. "We can't get too close, or we might start glowing again."

Marcus took a step back, but his eyes stayed on hers. "I was afraid you were gone."

"Gone where?" she asked. "What are—?"

"Before you say anything, I wanted you to have these." He shoved an envelope in her hand. "Open it."

Lena carefully undid the flap and peered inside. "*A Midsummer Night's Dream* tickets?"

"At the Blue Hills Theater, like the production you saw when you were younger."

"Oh," she said, closing the envelope. "Connie didn't want to go after all?"

"Connie?"

"It's fine, Marcus. You didn't have to do this." She handed the envelope back to him.

He made a strange sound in the back of his throat. "I can't believe this," he said. "Isn't anything ever good enough for you?"

"What are you talking about?"

"I've been killing myself trying to make everything perfect for you, and you don't even care!" he cried. "I mean, look at my eyes!"

When she looked, she was surprised to see how dry and bloodshot his normally twinkling eyes were. "What happened?"

"That's what I get for trying to smell nice for you!" he cried. "Maybe the future really does happen for a reason. Maybe we should be apart."

Lena gasped. "Are you breaking up with me?" She'd known something would have to change after Natalie had told her about the flirting, but Lena hadn't expected this. She'd foolishly thought they could find a way to work things out.

Marcus only looked at his feet. Then he walked away

without a word. Clearly, he thought there was no point in trying anymore.

Marcus's head throbbed as he walked home from Lena's. "Are you breaking up with me?" she'd asked, and he hadn't been able to answer. What was there to say? Of course he didn't want them to break up, but if she was moving and Natalie had seen a future in which they were apart, maybe there was no point in fighting anymore. And what more could he do? He'd gotten those tickets for her thinking she'd see how much she meant to him, and she'd shot him down.

He froze when he rounded the corner and saw Caspar Brown waiting for him in front of his house, the familiar jolt of fear zipping through him. Then Marcus remembered that he'd been the one to ask for the meeting in the first place.

"So, do you have it?" Caspar asked.

Marcus sighed and pulled the model robot out of his backpack. He'd carefully wrapped it in bubble wrap, trying not to think about the fact that he'd never see it again. He couldn't believe he was doing this. He'd needed the money to pay his mom back for the play tickets, and now Lena didn't even want to go. But a deal was a deal. He'd promised Caspar the robot, so he had to deliver.

Caspar took a look through the plastic and nodded. "I thought you said this one wasn't for sale," he said.

"I changed my mind."

Marcus cringed as Caspar shoved the robot into his bag like it was a pair of gym socks. He didn't care that it had taken weeks to restore the model, or that Grandpa Joe had been there the whole time, encouraging Marcus but letting him do it all on his own.

"Well, thanks," Caspar said, turning to go.

"Wait, where's my money?"

Caspar shrugged his rounded shoulders. "Sorry. I gave you all I had last time."

"But this one is worth twice as much! You can't take it!"

Caspar grinned. "Why not?"

"Because I'll...I'll send the creature after you again. You know what I'm talking about."

He could see Caspar hesitate for a second, fear flashing across his face as he remembered the ghost cat attacking him. But then he smirked. "I'm not scared of that thing. If it was even real," he announced. Then he rushed off, glancing over his shoulder like he was on the lookout for the cat. Clearly he *was* scared of it, but not enough to keep him from stealing something he wanted.

"No!" Marcus cried, rushing after Caspar. "Give it back!"

But Caspar was already halfway up the street, and even if he did catch up to him, Marcus couldn't exactly wrestle the model away from a guy twice his size. Even though Caspar's fists hadn't touched him this time, he still felt beaten down. How could he have been so stupid? He'd given up one of his most precious possessions for nothing.

chapter 28

T hat night, Marcus kicked *Quilting for Beginners* under his bed and started working on restoring a new model, trying to forget about the gaping hole in his collection that he could never fill. But before he could figure out which pieces of the model were missing, his sister threw open his bedroom door with so much force that it rattled his worktable.

"Have you ever heard of knocking?"

"What on earth did you tell Peter Chung at the meet today?"

He gulped. He'd known it was only a matter of time before his disastrous conversation with Peter got back to his sister, but he'd been foolishly hoping Peter might forget all about it.

"How could you tell him that I'd never had a boyfriend?" she demanded.

"You don't understand!" Marcus said, scrambling to get out of his chair. "When I told him you liked him, he got really excited."

"You told him *what*?" Ann-Marie roared. In that instant,

she sounded exactly like their dad did when his favorite hockey team was losing on TV.

Marcus shrunk back. "I didn't mean to. And I took it back right away and told him that you didn't."

Ann-Marie's eyes looked like they might pop out of her head. "Why would you do that? Why would you say any of that stuff to him, especially after I told you to stay away from him? Are you trying to ruin my life?"

"No, I was trying to make it better!" He knew how stupid that sounded, but what else could he say? "I think you and Peter would be perfect for each other. I was trying to—"

"How many times do I have to tell you? *I don't want your help!*"

She thundered out of his room, and a second later, her bedroom door slammed shut, the thud echoing through the entire house. After that, there was a long silence. Then he heard it, a soft whimpering sound coming through the wall. His sister was crying.

Ann-Marie never cried. Like their dad, she thought it was the ultimate sign of weakness. No matter how injured she was from running or how upset she was about the rare bad grade, she never cried. Marcus had sometimes wondered if her eyes even had tear ducts.

But now she wasn't just crying. She was sobbing. And it was his fault.

Suddenly, the ghost cat was at Marcus's side, batting at him with a glowing paw. Then it jumped off his bed and bolted out into the hallway. Marcus watched as the cat crept toward Ann-Marie's room and pawed at her door a few times. He thought he heard the faintest scratching sound, almost like a real cat would make.

Clearly, Ann-Marie heard it too, because her door opened a crack. Seeing its chance, the ghost cat darted into the room right before Ann-Marie shut the door again.

Marcus had thought the cat hated Ann-Marie, but it seemed to know that she needed some comfort. He could picture it curled up on the bed beside her, nuzzling her while she cried. He didn't know if his sister could feel its warm presence beside her, but he wished more than anything that she could.

As Marcus stumbled out of second period in a fog the next day, he was surprised to get a message from Mr. Perris on his phone. Have you seen Lena? She never made it to school. Her mother hasn't heard from her, and her bike is still here.

The words swam in front of his eyes. Lena was missing? He instantly replayed their awful conversation yesterday. Was it his fault she was gone? He dialed Lena's number, his fingers shaking, but she didn't pick up.

He ran through the hallway toward Natalie's locker, managing to catch her as she was walking away. "Lena's gone!" he cried. "Her dad can't find her. Do you have any idea where she might be?"

Natalie shook her head. "Have you talked to Eddie? He should be able to track her down."

Right. Eddie. Why hadn't he thought of that? He left Eddie a message, praying his boss called him back right away.

Marcus couldn't even think about going to English. Instead, he went to the nurse's office and pretended to be sick. It wasn't hard, considering that his head was pounding and he was so jittery that he thought he might throw up. Where could Lena be? If her bike was still at her house, did that mean she'd gone somewhere on foot? Or by bus?

As he waited for his mom in the school lobby, he tried calling Lena again, and this time he heard a click after the first ring.

"Lena?" he asked. "Are you there?"

In the background, he thought he heard muffled squeaking, like something was being hoisted up on a pulley. Then there was another click, and the call ended.

Marcus frantically redialed the number, but it went straight to voice mail.

His mind raced. What had that squeaking sound been? He knew he'd heard it before, but where?

Something in his brain clicked. He was almost positive that it was the sound of a theater curtain being drawn. He'd heard it plenty of times during play rehearsal. Encouraged, he ran into the auditorium and scanned the stage and the wings, but there was no one there.

Marcus went back to the lobby and slumped onto a bench. Clearly, his mind was playing tricks on him. Besides, why would Lena come to school and hide out in the auditorium? It would only remind her of everything that had happened with *Alice*.

Suddenly, he thought of the Blue Hills Theater. Even though Lena had flat-out rejected the tickets he'd gotten her, Marcus was suddenly convinced that that's where she'd gone. After all, it was where Lena had first realized she wanted to be an actress. Considering that her dreams of being one had been crushed, maybe she'd needed to go back there.

When his mom came to pick him up, Marcus waited until they were in the car and then begged her to take him to the theater.

"That's a half hour drive away!" she said. "If you suspect Lena's there, you should tell her father."

"But I could be wrong. Can't we go to the theater and check? I think it might be my fault she ran off in the first place."

His mom sighed. "This girl means a lot to you, doesn't she?"

"She's…she's the best, Mom." Even after everything, Lena was still his match. She was the only person he could really laugh with, and he knew that if he needed her help, she'd be there in an instant. He wouldn't have given up his robot model for anyone else.

His mom finally nodded and turned the car toward the highway. "But don't think you can pull something like this again, okay? Next time I get a call from your school saying you're sick, you better be on death's door."

He wanted to hug her for trusting him on this. He only hoped that he was right.

⇻ **chapter 29** →

Lena sat in the empty theater, on the stage where she'd seen her first real play. The space looked smaller than she remembered it, but she could still picture the actors in their elaborate costumes, spouting Shakespearean language in a way that was both foreign and mesmerizing.

She heard voices out in the hallway and froze. She'd managed to sneak into the theater when the woman at the box office wasn't looking, but it was only a matter of time before she was discovered. She wasn't even sure what she was doing here, only that she'd needed to get away from everything so that she could think.

After a minute, the voices faded again. Lena sighed in relief.

She lay back on the stage and closed her eyes, the stage lights making the insides of her eyelids glow pink. What if she'd gone along with Mr. Jackson's silly exercises? Would she still be in the play now? Would Connie Reynolds's wrist still be intact, or would she have found another way to wheedle her way in between Lena and Marcus?

When Marcus had called her a few minutes earlier, she'd answered it, almost ready to talk to him. Almost, but not quite. Because suddenly she'd imagined him saying that he wanted them to stay broken up, and the thought had been too painful to bear. So she'd hung up on him and turned off her phone instead.

Maybe going with her mom was the best option. She could start over at a new school, try out for the play there, and maybe do things the right way for once. Maybe she could even figure out how to make things right between her and Marcus again. Or what had gone wrong in the first place.

She took in a long breath and tried to calm her emotions, the way she'd done when Marcus was using his powers.

And suddenly she smelled it. Buttered popcorn. That was weird. This wasn't a movie theater after all. And the concession stand was closed today anyway.

She sat up, sniffing the air. Sure enough, the smell wafted toward her again. It was coming from the wings.

Lena got to her feet and slowly followed the scent until she got to the costume closet. She pulled it open and gasped when she saw a clump of light hovering in between the musty suits.

"Mr. Watts?" She couldn't believe it. Her mom's weird soul-tracking trick had been right! "What are you doing here?"

The ball of light didn't react for a second, only stayed there glowing. Finally, she heard Mr. Watts's voice. "This was the first place I ever performed."

Lena's mind blurred, and for just a moment, she saw this stage many years ago as a group of teenagers in funny clothes put on a variety show. Mr. Watts, about fifty years younger, was prancing around the stage like a horse while the audience laughed hysterically. Then the memory faded, but Lena was left with a sense of warmth and comfort in her chest.

"I love this place too," Lena told him. "I saw my first real play here." She laughed sadly. "My boyfriend—ex-boyfriend—even got us tickets to see it here again, but I think that was only out of pity for me getting kicked out of my school play." She didn't know why she was telling a lost soul all of this. It felt even worse to say it out loud.

The ball of light drifted toward her and hovered near her shoulder. It bounced up and down like a tennis ball, and Lena had the impression that it was trying to cheer her up.

"Mr. Watts, I know you feel happy here, but it's time for you to move on."

The ball backed away slightly. This wasn't working. She had to try something else. "You know Viv, your student? She raves about you all the time. And she said you loved playing pranks when you were younger because they made you feel alive. I bet that's why you've been playing all those pranks on me now, right?"

The ball didn't move, but she could tell it was listening. Encouraged, Lena kept talking. "But if you're a performer, then you have to know when to close the curtain and end the show." She closed her eyes for a moment, unable to believe the words that were about to come out of her mouth. "You have to trust the process."

The ball of light drooped in defeat. Then it slowly drifted toward her.

As if they knew exactly what to do, Lena's fingers flared to life with a deep-purple light. Maybe that meant Marcus was calm wherever he was. Or, Lena realized with a jolt, now that they'd broken up like Eddie had suggested, the link between them was gone. Their powers were free again.

Lena should have been happy at the thought, but she only felt worse. That meant things between her and Marcus were really over.

But she pushed all of that way. "You'll be happy where you're going," she told Mr. Watts. "Think of all the people there that you can play tricks on."

She thought she heard a faint chuckle as the light drifted toward her hand. And then, as it was about to touch her finger, it hesitated. And backed up.

"No, Mr. Watts!" she said. "It's okay. Let go!"

But it was too late.

"Your shoe's untied," the faint voice said with a cackle. Then the light zipped back into the wings and was gone.

chapter 30

Lena frantically searched the wings for Mr. Watts, but it was no use. She'd been so close, but he'd disappeared. Again. She nearly let out a scream of frustration, but voices sounded in the hallway, and she hurried into the costume closet instead. A second later, one of the theater doors creaked open, and she could hear a muffled conversation moving toward her.

"She's in here," someone said.

Lena sighed. She'd been found.

Would they arrest her for trespassing? She couldn't imagine what her parents would say to that. Her dad would probably have her head scanned to see if he could spot a pattern in her brain that explained her rebellious behavior.

After a minute, she heard footsteps coming up the stage steps. Then a voice she recognized said, "She should be here somewhere."

It was Eddie.

Lena closed her eyes and nestled deeper into a scratchy lace gown. Of course her boss had been able to track her down. If he knew where her assignments were supposed to be before they happened, surely he had a way of keeping tabs on his employees too.

She tried not to breathe as she heard Eddie walking around on the stage. It was silly to hide from him, but she didn't want to deal with anyone right now.

"Dad, do you want me to check in the wings?" a girl's voice called out.

"Sure. You take that side," Eddie called back. "I'll take this one."

Huh? Since when was Eddie someone's father? And why did the girl's voice sound familiar?

Lena sunk as far back into the closet as she could as light footsteps came closer. And then, through the crack in the door, Lena saw her. Natalie.

"No one here!" Natalie called back. "Are you sure your info is right?"

"The info is always correct. She must be here. Lena, can you hear me? We want to make sure you're all right. Your family is worried about you."

"Dad, look!" Natalie suddenly called. "Her bag is on the seat over there!"

This didn't make any sense. How could Eddie and Natalie be related?

She heard them walking around and around the theater for a few minutes. Finally, Eddie let out a loud, frustrated sigh. "It looks like we missed her."

"What do we do if Marcus finds her first?" Natalie's voice sounded lower-pitched than usual, not to mention more serious and worried. No wonder Lena hadn't recognized it when she'd first heard it in the theater.

"We deal with it," Eddie said. "But the longer we can keep those two apart, the better."

Lena sucked in a dusty breath that nearly made her cough. What were they talking about?

"If you had done your job correctly, this would not be an issue," Eddie added.

"I tried!" Natalie said. "I did everything you said, and it seemed like she was going to go to Arizona and the whole problem would be over."

Eddie sighed. "We will figure it out."

"But what if we can't break them up for good?" Natalie asked. "The last future I saw said they'd be apart, but what if it changes again?"

"All right, let me go call the boss lady and see what she wants us to do." He walked off the stage, leaving Natalie standing there alone. A minute later, Lena heard the theater door creak open again as Eddie went out into the hallway.

Lena's brain felt like it was too big for her head. Not only was Natalie Eddie's daughter, but she'd been assigned to break Lena and Marcus up? And had Natalie actually said that she could *see the future*?

Suddenly, Lena didn't care about being discovered. She wanted answers. She pushed her way out of the closet and marched over to Natalie, brushing a coating of dust off her clothes.

Natalie jumped at the sight of her. "Lena! How much did you hear?"

"Enough to know you've been lying to me since the second I met you. You're Eddie's daughter? So all that stuff you said about wanting to reconnect with your dad was a lie?"

"It wasn't a lie. I only met him a few weeks ago, and when he said he had a job I could help him with, I took it in exchange for being able to come live with him."

"And the job was getting me and Marcus to break up? Why would you agree to do something like that? And what's all this about you seeing the future?"

"Marcus didn't tell you that I'm a seer?" Natalie asked.

Lena gaped at her. He knew something like that and didn't tell her? *Focus*, Lena told herself. *That's not important right now.* "So whatever you saw in the future made you convinced that Marcus and I had to break up?"

Natalie nodded. "It was like that haunted hospital times ten. I saw people losing their abilities for days, souls wandering away and getting harder to catch, and people doing crazier and crazier things for love. Dangerous stuff."

"Like hanging off skyscrapers to profess their love for each other?" Lena asked, suddenly remembering the woman she'd seen on the news.

Natalie nodded. "Tons of people like that all over the world, all because of the link between your powers. When I told my dad about my vision, he was afraid that if the connection between you and Marcus grew any stronger, he'd never be able to separate it. And when he tried to convince you guys to break up, you refused."

"So he sent you in to mess with us. Was all that stuff you said about Marcus flirting with you and Connie even true?"

"No." Natalie lowered her eyes. "I didn't want to lie to you about things, but I thought it was the only way."

"So you lied about other stuff too?" Lena asked, her mind whirling. "Were you even in *Alice in Wonderland*?" She gasped. "Are you even a soul collector?"

Natalie's silence was all the answer she needed. Lena couldn't believe it. She'd opened up to Natalie from the minute she'd met her, amazed at herself for trusting someone so easily, and now it turned out she'd been an idiot to believe a word out of the girl's mouth.

Just then, Eddie came back into the theater. "So you *are* here," he said. He didn't sound surprised, only tired and sad.

"Eddie, what is going on?" Lena asked. "And tell me the *truth* this time!"

He ran his hand through his graying hair. Now that Lena knew he was Natalie's father, she realized they had the same dark eyes.

"I knew from the time you and Marcus swapped your powers that they were linked, but I did not know how they would affect each other. I thought if I brought Natalie in to weaken the connection between you two, we could end this before it became a problem. But I was wrong. Your feelings for each other are too strong, and they're clouding your judgment."

"My judgment is fine!" Lena cried.

"Lena," he said softly, "I know firsthand how badly things can go when emotions interfere with the order of things. I could not let it happen again."

"Again?" Lena asked. "What are you talking about?"

"Tell her about the probation, Dad," Natalie said. "Maybe that will make her understand."

Eddie sighed. "It was years ago, back when I was still

a matchmaker. If the boss lady had not intervened in time, things could have been a disaster."

"But what happened?" Lena asked.

"It...it's not my story to tell. Or at least, it's not only my story. Someone else was also involved, and I am not sure she would want you to know the truth, Lena."

"Why would some random person care if I knew the truth?"

"Because," Eddie said with a soft sigh, "the other person involved is your mother."

chapter 31

On the drive to the theater, Marcus tried to pay attention as his mom described a new trash sculpture she was working on, but his head was swimming. What would he say to Lena when he saw her? Would she even want to talk to him?

Suddenly, he heard a faint "meow" from the backseat. At first, he was sure he'd imagined it. But then it came again, more insistent this time. "Mrow!"

Marcus oh-so-casually glanced over his shoulder and bit back a smile. Sure enough, the ghost cat was curled up in the backseat of the car. Apparently, it had gotten bored waiting for him at home and had decided to go for a ride.

"What are you looking at?" his mom asked after a minute. "Is that old takeout container still back there?"

"Um, no," Marcus said. "It's nothing."

His mom gave him a long look before focusing her eyes back on the road. "Are you sure you're okay? You've seemed so distracted recently. Is this because of Lena? I thought things were going well with you two."

"They were," he said. "It's complicated."

To his surprise, his mom laughed. "Oh yes, relationships are the definition of complicated. Look at your father and me."

"How can you...stand him sometimes?" He'd never dared say something like that to his mom before, but he'd often wondered it. His dad could be okay, but he was so stubborn and demanding. It made Marcus crazy.

"He's always been a little rough around the edges," his mom said. "To be honest, sometimes we drive each other batty. But he's also the man I fell in love with, even if we don't always see eye to eye on things." She laughed again. "On *most* things."

"But wouldn't it be so much easier if you had things in common? I mean, you don't know anything about sports, and Dad never understands any of your sculptures. How can that even work?"

"You and Lena don't need to do all the same things, do you? You can have your own interests and still have plenty to talk about."

Marcus thought back to how much of his own life he'd cast aside recently to spend more time doing what Lena wanted, not because she'd expected him to but because he'd thought that's what he was supposed to do.

"So you mean I didn't have to read all that stuff about quilting and watch all those boring recordings of plays?" he asked.

His mom chuckled. "The last time you sat through a whole play, I think you were about three years old, and it was a five-minute-long puppet show. You were always more interested in building things than in watching them."

"I want me and Lena to be like Grandpa Joe and Grandma Lily. They were made for each other. When they first started dating, everything was perfect."

His mom gave him a strange look. "Marcus, how much do you remember about your grandmother?"

"Bits and pieces, I guess." Most of his memories of Grandma Lily were from Grandpa's stories about her.

"My mother was a lovely woman, but she could also be a nightmare." His mom laughed, remembering. "She would boss your grandpa around like he was a hired hand."

"She did?"

His mom pitched her voice up an octave. "'Joe, hold my purse. Joe, go to the store and pick up some of that cheese I like. Joe, stop breathing so loud. I'm trying to watch the news.'" She laughed again, her voice going back to normal. "It drove the rest of us insane, but he shrugged it off. He said their relationship had been like that since they'd met, and he wasn't going to change a thing."

"But...but Grandpa always said they were perfect for each other."

"They were," his mom said. "But that didn't make them perfect people."

Marcus gazed out the car window as blurs of houses flew by. He thought about how things with Lena had been going wrong for days. Despite all that, he knew she was the one he was supposed to be with. Maybe Grandpa had felt the same way, even if it meant putting up with some of Grandma Lily's orders. Grandpa hadn't cruised through his relationship. He'd made it work.

"Mom, can we stop somewhere so I can get flowers for Lena?" he asked. This time he'd be sure to get the non-allergy-inducing kind.

His mom gave him a warm smile. "Of course."

They pulled over at the next exit and stopped at a small grocery store. The instant Marcus opened his car door—*zoom!*—the ghost cat leaped over his lap and darted out of the car.

"No!" Marcus cried. He instinctively tried to grab it—even though his fingers would have gone right through anyway—but the cat was already disappearing among the other cars parked in the lot.

"Are you okay?" his mom asked as he jumped out of the car and started to hurry after the cat. "Marcus!"

"I'll be right back, Mom!" he yelled over his shoulder. He chased the ball of light across the pavement, but it was nearly impossible to see it in the bright sun. Finally, he reached the doors of the supermarket and stood there, not sure where to go.

Then he heard a "meow" nearby. He tiptoed to the side of the building and peered down an alley lined with trash bins. "Meow," he heard again, but this time it was a much deeper sound. A second later, he saw a big, fluffy cat—a live one—strutting down the alley. And trotting behind it, glowing as brightly as ever, was the ghost cat.

Marcus stared as the two of them circled around each other and then intertwined tails. If his powers worked on ghost animals, he was sure he'd see love sparks dancing between them. It was the most unlikely pair he could have imagined, but the two cats seemed perfectly content together as they let out a joyful "mrow!" in unison and scampered down the alley.

He thought he saw the ghost cat give him one last glance, and then it was gone. Marcus stood there for a long minute, listening, but he didn't hear anything else.

He sighed and headed back toward the store entrance. Clearly, this was where the ghost cat wanted to be. Marcus had never thought he'd become so attached to the creature, but as he walked away, he had to swallow the tightness in his throat.

He was going to miss that little ball of light, but he was glad it had found its match. Now it was time for Marcus to track down his.

chapter 32

Lena stared at Eddie. "My mom?" she repeated. That couldn't be right. What did her mom have to do with this? But then she remembered what her mom had said about knowing Eddie in college and about something nearly ending their friendship. "If you're doing all this because of stuff that happened with my mom, I think I have a right to know about it!"

Eddie scratched at his beard. Then he glanced down the hall, and a strange expression passed over his face. "I suppose we can ask her."

Lena turned to see her mom standing at the end of the hall. "Hello, Eddie," she said in little more than a whisper.

"Jessica." He looked like he wanted to rush over and give her a hug, but he held back. Clearly, it had been a long time since they'd seen each other.

"Mom, what are you doing here?" Lena asked.

"When your father told me you were missing, I started

listing the places you could be, and this old theater popped into my head. I thought it was worth a try."

Wow. Her mom knew her better than Lena had thought. "What is Eddie talking about? What happened to put him on probation?"

Lena's mom sighed. "I suppose there's no point in trying to hide the truth any longer. It was years ago, Lena, before you were even born. Eddie was only trying to help me." She smoothed her short hair behind her ears, like she was trying to compose herself for whatever truth she was about to spill. "When your father and I met, he was so focused on his research and on his career that he didn't even notice me. But there was something about him. I knew I had to have him. So...I asked Eddie to help me."

Lena stared at her boss. "You zapped a couple even though they weren't a match?"

Eddie nodded solemnly. "I was new to this country, and Jessica was the only friend I had." The way he talked about her mom made Lena wonder if he'd once thought of her as more than a friend. "When she asked me to help her, I could not say no, even though it was against the rules. After I matched her with Ken, at first everything seemed all right. But then..."

"Other people's assignments started going wrong,"

Lena's mom explained. "We had no idea it was our fault. But eventually they traced it back to what Eddie had done, and he got in trouble for it. I…I'd like to say that I told them the truth, about how I'd begged him to help me, but I didn't. He was stripped of his role as matchmaker and given a desk job, and I got to marry the man I'd tricked into loving me. After that, I wasn't sure Eddie could ever forgive me."

"It took me a long time," he admitted. "I blamed you for what happened, but the truth is it was my decision to make."

"So you and Dad…" Lena shook her head in disbelief. "You were never meant to be together?"

Her mom smiled sadly. "Your father is a good man. Even after the spark between us faded, he stayed with me. I think he even grew to care about me. And then you came along, Lena, and we were so happy. But I couldn't forget the fact that I'd deceived him. Eventually, it was too much. I thought he would be happier—you both would be—if I wasn't there."

Lena thought about how her dad had already been forced into love twice. Once by Eddie and again when Lena had tried to make him fall in love with Marguerite. It seemed so unfair that other people kept controlling his emotions. Was it different this time with Viv?

"Do you see now why I had to do something before the link

between your powers became too dangerous?" Eddie asked. "That link had already started affecting other people's abilities, and the more emotional you became, the worse it got."

"And now?" Lena asked. "My powers seem to be working better again, and we stopped shooting sparks at each other."

Eddie sighed. "Then perhaps our plan is finally working," he said, but he didn't sound convinced.

As Lena got her bag, knowing it was time to head home, her entire body felt heavy. The problem was fixed, wasn't it? She and Marcus had broken up, and everything was going to go back to normal again. But it didn't feel like a solution. It felt like some kind of cruel joke.

When Marcus's mom finally pulled up in front of the Blue Hills Theater, Marcus threw open the car door and hurried inside. The place was deserted except for a bored-looking woman at the box office.

"Can I help you?" she droned, barely glancing up from a thick book of one-act plays.

"I'm looking for my, um, girlfriend." He didn't need to get into his complicated relationship status with a total stranger.

The woman shook her head. "No shows today, so no one's here. If you come back tomorrow—"

"Tomorrow will be too late!" he cried, waving his bouquet of daisies around.

"Go look around if you don't believe me," the woman said flatly. "But I told you. There's no one here."

Marcus dashed into the theater, but the stage was empty. He poked around every room and hallway he could find, but the woman was right. There was no one there.

Finally, he had to admit that it was hopeless. On his way out of the theater, he deposited the bouquet at the box office. "Enjoy," he told the woman, and her face brightened a little at the gesture. At least the flowers had done someone some good.

As Marcus slunk back to his mom's car, he was furious at himself for being so wrong. Maybe he didn't know Lena as well as he'd thought.

chapter 33

Do you want to stop and get some lunch on the way back?" Lena's mom asked as they got into the car. Lena hadn't wanted a ride home, but her mom wouldn't take no for an answer.

"That's okay."

They sat in silence for nearly half an hour, listening to a radio station that played one overly cheerful pop song after another. Lena tried to process everything she'd learned about her parents and about Natalie, but it hurt her brain to even think about it. Eventually, all she could manage was staring blankly out the window.

Finally, her mom turned down the music. "Are we going to talk about what happened?"

"If you want," Lena said, pretending to be interested in the buttons on the car door.

"I have to go back to Arizona in a couple of days, and I want us to work things out before I go. I wish I didn't have to leave, but my boss is threatening to fire me if I take any more time off."

Lena didn't answer. Of course her mom was leaving again. That's what she did after all.

"I know you're angry with me," her mom went on. "I've kept a lot from you and I'm sorry."

"That's it?" Lena clicked the locks shut and then unlocked them again, the sound oddly soothing in her ears. "You lie to me for years, and that's all you can say?"

"I didn't want to lie to you! You know the rules about our powers. And how could I possibly tell you the truth about what I did to your father? You idolize that man."

"Because he doesn't hide things from me. Because he doesn't abandon me!"

"Lena—"

"I bet the only reason Eddie called you after all these years was to try to get me to move out to Arizona. You were part of his stupid plan and didn't even know it."

Her mom started to object, but Lena didn't want to hear it. "Forget it. I don't want to talk about this anymore." She clicked the locks a few more times, but the soothing feeling was gone.

"You can't shut me out, Lena."

"Why not? You did it to me when you left!"

"Lena, trust me, I only—"

"Trust you?" Lena cried. "How can I trust you—or anyone—after all the stuff you've done?" Then she fell silent, suddenly remembering what Abigail had spat at her the other day: "The only person you trust is yourself." And then Lena remembered what Marcus had said about her being like her mom. She'd bristled at the thought, but maybe he'd been right. At least a little bit.

She expected her mom to argue, but instead she only said, "I know, honey. And I'm sorry. But I promise that if you give me a chance, I'll spend every day from now on trying to make it up to you. I know that means trusting me, at least a little, even if I don't deserve it. Can you do that?"

Lena looked down at her lap. *Could* she do that? She barely even trusted her dad to make a costume for her, and he was the one person who'd always been there for her. And Marcus…she'd wanted to trust him, but the minute Natalie had told her those lies about him, she'd believed them. No wonder Eddie had said they were on different frequencies. How could she ever really be in sync with someone she didn't have total faith in?

"I think I screwed up, Mom," she said softly, surprised to feel tears prickling at the corners of her eyes.

"I did too, honey," her mom said. "But all we can do is try

to make up for the things we did and hope they'll go better next time."

Lena looked out the window. When it came to Marcus, she wasn't sure there would be a next time.

Marcus pored over the email Lena had sent him, looking for any sign that she missed him. But the email was all business. It described what Lena had found out about Eddie's past with her mom, and it explained how Natalie and Eddie had been trying to break them up. Funny how Natalie had claimed that you couldn't change the future, but she'd been trying to do just that. Clearly, she'd lied about lots of things.

Marcus couldn't believe all of that had happened, and that it had been at the Blue Hills Theater. He'd been right about Lena going there after all, and if the ghost cat hadn't run out of the car, he might have even made it there in time to see her. But it didn't seem to matter. Lena had only ended the email with "I thought you should know." No "I miss you" or even a formal "Sincerely." That's how little she cared.

He supposed Eddie had to be pretty relieved right about now. Not only had Marcus and Lena broken up—like Natalie had foreseen—but the emotional connection between them was practically nonexistent. Even if they were on different frequencies, it didn't matter anymore. The balance of the universe was safe. So why did things feel so awful?

A knock came on his door, and his sister poked her head in. "Can I come in?"

"Since when do you ask first?"

She didn't answer. Instead, she came to sit on his bed. He expected the ghost cat to scamper away from his sister like it always did, and then he remembered that it was gone. Funny how it had only been a part of his life—a very strange part—for a few weeks, and now the house seemed oddly empty without it. But he was also glad it was out there somewhere, living its happy ending. At least someone got to.

"Mom got a call from Lena's dad," his sister said. "I guess they found her. She was with her mom."

"I heard." He'd been relieved when Hayleigh had told him the news, but he'd also been a little angry that Lena had let them all worry about her.

"And, um, I'm sorry about you and Lena," she added. "Mom said you broke up? That's too bad. I liked her."

Was it possible his sister was actually feeling some sympathy toward him? Maybe she hadn't had enough water today and was delirious from dehydration.

"Oh and here," she said. "I found this at a yard sale down

the street. They mostly had used toasters and other junk, but I saw this and thought you could…you know."

She shoved something at him, and it took Marcus a minute to realize it was a model fighter jet. It wasn't the kind of thing he normally worked on, but the fact that his sister had thought of him at all when she'd seen it was kind of amazing.

"Wow, thanks," he said, scanning his shelves. It still hurt to see the empty spot where the robot had been, but there was an open space beside it where the jet would fit perfectly.

Ann-Marie hesitated for a moment in his doorway and said, "I know you're like Grandpa, a total romantic." He expected her to roll her eyes, but instead she gave him the tiniest smile. "Don't worry. I'm sure you'll find the perfect person for you some day."

Marcus knew her words were intended to make him feel better, but they didn't. He didn't want to find someone else who was perfect for him. He'd already found her. She just didn't want him back.

chapter 34

On the opening night of *Alice*, instead of getting ready for the show like she would have been doing if she were still in the cast, Lena found herself walking Professor through Marcus's neighborhood.

Beside her, Professor wagged his tail nonstop, obviously excited about the extralong outing. He was also clearly enjoying having his squirrel wife tagging along. She was scampering in and out of the bushes and sometimes walking right beside him so it looked like Lena had both a pet dog and a pet woodland creature.

Lena wondered briefly if her mom had already landed in Arizona. She was glad the two of them had worked things out, but Lena wasn't sure she'd ever be ready to go live with her mom. At least there were no lies between them anymore. Maybe that meant they could learn to trust each other again.

When she reached Marcus's house, Lena didn't let herself glance at it as she rushed by. She definitely didn't want to make things even more awkward between them by lurking outside his window.

Once they were past Marcus's house, Professor insisted on stopping at a pond and sniffing every inch of icy mud while the squirrel scurried into a clump of bushes. Lena glanced around to make sure no one was watching, and then she focused on calling up her energy, just to see what would happen. She hadn't had any assignments the past few days, but she wasn't sure if that was Eddie's doing or if it was a slow soul-collecting week.

Her fingers gradually flared to life like they were waking up from a long nap. The purple glow around them was hazy and unsteady. After a minute, it went out on its own.

Lena let out a long sigh that seemed to echo in the crisp air. Her sluggish powers had to be a sign that Marcus was unhappy. It was bad enough that she was miserable. She didn't want him to be too. Maybe she *should* go stop by his house.

No, she told herself firmly. He'd made it clear he wanted a break from her. Going to see him now would only make things harder. Even though there was obviously still a link between them, no doubt it was fading by the day.

She turned to tell Professor that they were heading home, but she spotted a familiar face across the street. Caspar Brown.

He was standing in the middle of his driveway, leaning over

what looked like a couple of toys. Only they weren't toys, Lena realized. They were Marcus's models.

Lena gasped as Caspar picked up a rock larger than his meaty hand and lifted it over his head, clearly about to crush the models with it.

"Stop!" She took off running, Professor barking in alarm behind her. "What are you doing? You can't break those."

Caspar looked up at her and smirked. "Why not? They're mine."

"They're Marcus's. I've seen them in his room."

"Not anymore. He sold them to me," Caspar said.

"If you paid money for them, then why would you destroy them?" Lena asked.

"It's not my money," he said. "I took it out of my mom's purse. Besides, who cares? It's just old junk anyway."

But it wasn't junk, not to Marcus. "Why did he sell them to you?"

Caspar snorted. "Like you don't know."

"What are you talking about?"

"He sold them for some tickets or something. He was trying to impress you." He laughed. "What a loser. I didn't even pay him for the robot, and he was too chicken to do anything about it."

Lena's stomach went cold. Marcus had sold the models— his favorite models—for her? For the theater tickets that she'd thrown back in his face?

"Give them back," she said.

"Yeah, right." Caspar started to lift the rock again, but this time Lena grabbed his tree-trunk arm. She had to reach far over her head to hold on to it.

"I said, give them back," she said through her teeth. Beside her, Professor growled.

Caspar glanced uncertainly at the dog. "If your mutt attacks me, I'm calling the police."

"Good, call them," Lena said. "I'm sure they'd want to hear all about how you steal things."

"As if they care about people stealing small stuff like this," he said, clearly speaking from experience. "You can't prove anything anyway." Still, he let the rock drop to his feet, shaking his arm out of Lena's grasp. But when she went to pick up the models, Caspar stepped in her way. "Nope. These aren't going anywhere."

"If you don't give them back, I'll—"

But what could she do? Caspar was more than twice her size. And even if she could somehow use her powers to scare him off, they were too unstable now to be of any help.

"Yeah," Caspar said, smirking again. "Now go away before I call the police for the fun of it." He reached out and gave Lena's shoulder a shove.

Just then, Lena heard a familiar laugh behind her. Then a ball of light came charging over her shoulder. It was Mr. Watts.

"What the—?" Caspar cried as the ball of light flew at him. "Get it away from me!"

He turned to run, but it was too late. The ball of light swirled around him, and Lena watched with a mixture of horror and amusement as Caspar's oversized jeans suddenly slid down to his ankles, revealing boxers with pink hearts all over them.

Lena laughed in surprise. Caspar Brown had gotten pantsed by a ghost!

Caspar scrambled to pull his jeans up as he backed away, his eyes unnaturally wide. "What is it with you and that Marcus kid?" he spat. "Why are you both such freaks?"

Lena didn't answer. Instead, she watched in satisfaction as the ball of light started to charge at him again.

Caspar didn't wait another second. He turned and bolted into his house, leaving Marcus's models behind.

When he was gone, Lena grabbed the models and raced across the street to the pond. When she stopped, she found herself face-to-face with the ball of light.

"Thank you," she said. "You have no idea what a good thing you just did."

She heard Mr. Watts's faint voice say, "I never could stand a bully." Then he laughed. "Not a bad prank for my final act, eh?"

"Final act?" Lena asked. "Does that mean you're finally ready to move on?"

"Ready as I'll ever be," he said. The ball of light started to glow with a warmer, brighter light than ever before.

Lena's fingers flared to life. She reached out to touch the ball of light and heard Mr. Watts whisper, "Remember. Find your fun." Then her hand slowly sank into the clump of lights, and one by one, they went out like stars.

Then everything was still.

As Lena's hand stopped glowing, she felt the biggest sense of relief yet. And she knew that wherever Mr. Watts had gone, he was laughing like crazy.

She took in a deep breath and started to head for home, Professor trailing behind her. As she walked, she studied the models in her hands. She couldn't believe that after all the hours Marcus had put into restoring them, he would let someone like Caspar get his paws on them. And that he'd done it all for her.

chapter 35

It was the last indoor track meet before the holidays, and Marcus knew he was running out of chances to make things right with Ann-Marie and Peter. He had just enough time to pop in and talk to Peter before he had to go start setting things up for opening night of the play.

He spotted Ann-Marie warming up in the corner, running in place like a wind-up toy. "What do you want?" she asked when he went over.

"To wish you luck."

"And...?"

"And that's it. I know you'll be great."

"Oh," she said uncertainly, as if trying to figure out the catch. "Thanks."

When he went back to his seat, he waited for the first race to start. After a minute, as he'd hoped, Peter appeared in the corner. As usual, Claire was with him. Even though they were gazing adoringly into each other's eyes, the sparks between them looked more bored than ever before. When he squinted, Marcus could see a flash of drab green around them, like their auras had caught the flu.

Marcus took a deep breath and went over to them. "Hey, Peter, can I talk to you alone for a second?"

Peter glanced at Claire uncertainly, as if he wasn't sure if he needed her permission, but finally he nodded.

When they'd put a little distance between them and Claire, Marcus cleared his throat and blurted, "I'm sorry about all that stuff I said about my sister the other day. I didn't know what I was talking about, and I shouldn't have butted into her life."

"Oh, it's okay. I mean, I'm with Claire and everything, so I guess it doesn't matter."

"Do you actually like Claire?" Marcus couldn't help asking.

The question seemed to surprise Peter. "Um, well..." He frowned, as if trying to figure out what the word "like" meant.

"I know it's none of my business," Marcus said, "but you guys don't seem to have much to talk about. And, I mean, shouldn't you be able to say that you like your girlfriend?" After all, Marcus and his girlfriend weren't even technically together anymore, but he still liked her.

"Yeah," Peter said. "I guess you're right."

"And you can't say that about Claire, can you?"

"Sure I can. I like…" Peter frowned as the words obviously didn't want to come out of his mouth. "Huh, that's weird."

"Maybe that's something to think about," Marcus said. "By the way, are you going to the play tonight?"

"Not sure. Why?"

"Oh, no reason," Marcus said, trying to sound casual. "I think my sister's going, so I wondered if you were too. Well, anyway. See ya."

Then he forced himself to walk away. Even though he wanted to beg Peter to dump Claire. Even though he was desperate to convince him how perfect he and Ann-Marie were for each other. Even though there were dozens of tactics in Grandpa's dating book that he hadn't tried yet. He had to let it go and trust that a little spark of doubt might be enough to finally get Peter to realize the truth for himself.

Marcus went back to the bleachers and sat down as Ann-Marie's first race started. He couldn't believe how incredible she was, so driven and determined. She was a lot like their dad in that way. Or maybe, Marcus suddenly realized, in some ways that made her a lot like him.

Since Lena couldn't ride her bike while wearing her playing card costume, she asked her dad for a lift to school.

"Did Mr. Jackson change his mind about letting you be in the play?" her dad asked.

"Nope," Lena said. "But I need to go talk to Marcus."

He and Viv exchanged puzzled looks, probably wondering why she couldn't simply call him, but they didn't press. Instead, the three of them piled in the car, with the playing card costume strapped in next to Lena, and headed for the school.

"That's quite the costume," Viv said. "Did you make that, Ken?"

He beamed. "How can you tell?"

Viv gave Lena a knowing smile over her shoulder. "Oh, no reason."

Lena couldn't help smiling back. The costume looked more like a beehive than a playing card. Somehow all the pieces had come together honeycomb style, creating something more spherical than flat. She'd wanted to make a backup costume, but with everything else going on, she hadn't had time. Now it didn't matter anyway. The costume only needed to be good enough to get her backstage.

When they got to the school, Lena's dad headed off to show Viv how much the building had changed since he'd been a student there. Lena found herself smiling when she saw them walking away holding hands. She'd worried that her dad had been set up with yet another person who wasn't right for him, but Viv wasn't like that. Lena had to admit that this time, Eddie and whoever he worked for had finally gotten it right.

When she peered into the drama room, the first person she saw was Hayleigh.

"Lena!" she said with a gasp. "What are you doing here? Mr. Jackson will freak out if he sees you."

"Where is he?"

"The pipe that burst over Thanksgiving started leaking again," she said. "He's been with the custodians trying to fix it." She crinkled her nose. "What are you wearing?"

"My costume," Lena said. "Have you seen Marcus?"

But Hayleigh didn't answer, because just then, Abigail and Emery walked in, arm in arm.

"Are they together now?" Lena asked. Did that mean Emery had finally chosen between her friends?

"No," Hayleigh said. "Abigail and I decided to share him. She has him for the next seven minutes, and then I get to have him until quarter past."

Lena stared at her. "And you're okay with that?"

"What else am I supposed to do? It's the only way I can get any alone time with him!"

This was ridiculous. Lena didn't know why the sparks between her friends and Emery were as strong as ever, but the whole fiasco had to end. She grabbed Hayleigh's arm and pulled her over to Abigail and Emery.

"We need to settle this now," she said.

"Settle what?" asked Abigail.

"Emery," Lena said. "Do you like Abigail or Hayleigh, I mean really like them?"

"Sure," he said. "They're great."

"No, not great. I mean, do you get tingly when you see them and when they hold your hand? Can you laugh about eating expensive slime together? Do you know without a doubt that they're your perfect match and that you're meant to be together?"

Emery faltered, and the weird dreamy look on his face seemed to dim a notch. "N-no."

The other girls gasped. "What?" Hayleigh cried. "But we're perfect for each other!"

"Why?" Lena asked. "What makes him so great?"

Hayleigh opened her mouth to answer, but nothing came out. Lena turned to Abigail and asked her the same question, but she was also at a loss.

"Wait," Emery said suddenly. "Why would we be eating expensive slime?"

Lena laughed. "I have to go find Marcus."

"He's backstage," Abigail said. "He had to help move the sets so they wouldn't get wet."

"I need to talk to him."

"Can't it wait?" Abigail asked. "The show's about to start."

Lena saw that people were getting into places. But no, it couldn't wait, she realized. Suddenly, she knew exactly how that crazy lady dangling from a skyscraper must have felt when she'd scrawled "I love you, Bob." Marcus was right. Sometimes you needed a big romantic gesture to show the other person how you feel.

chapter 36

The trees were sopping wet. Marcus had spent hours and hours painting them, and now they were soggy, dripping messes thanks to the leaking pipe backstage. To be honest, the sets hadn't looked that much better when they'd been dry. Marcus was clearly not cut out for all this theater stuff. Funny how he'd only agreed to do it in the first place to spend more time with Lena, and now she wasn't even here.

When he and some of the other tech kids had finished blotting the sets with paper towels, a red-faced Mr. Jackson announced that it was already fifteen minutes past curtain and the show had to go on, soggy sets or not.

Marcus ignored his damp clothes and went to wait in the wings for intermission when he'd have to lug the wet trees back into the hallway. As the play started, he glanced around the auditorium through a crack in the curtain and spotted a familiar face in the crowd. Ann-Marie. He squinted and realized that sitting next to her, amazingly, was Peter Chung. Claire, on the other hand, was nowhere in sight.

Marcus couldn't believe it. Had his plan finally worked? He tried to detect any hint of a spark between Ann-Marie and Peter, but he didn't see anything in the darkness. He couldn't help feeling disappointed, but at least they were here together. Maybe the rest would come on its own. Either way, he was through interfering and trying to make things perfect. All that had done was drive Lena away. At least his sister's aura looked much less drab than it had a couple days ago. That was a start.

A few scenes later, he was barely paying attention to what was going on onstage, when he suddenly realized things were far too quiet.

He peeked onto the stage and spotted Emery Higgins in full Cheshire Cat gear, standing completely frozen with a pained expression on his painted face. The other kids onstage looked a bit panicked. Oh no. Emery had forgotten his lines!

Mr. Jackson was sitting in the front row, frantically waving at them to keep going, but no one seemed to know what to do. And then somewhere above the stage, someone let out a cry, and a second later, a giant beehive plummeted onto the stage.

It was the ultimate trust fall. Lena had to trust that she wouldn't plunge to her death. As she clung to a rope tied to the rafters, her feet dangling ten feet above the stage, her whole body screamed at her to go back to the safety of solid ground. She ignored it. If she wanted to show Marcus how serious she was about him, she had to go big. Maybe their powers would still be messed up, but at least he'd know how she felt.

So she gripped the paintbrush with one hand and the rope with the other, and she leaned toward the back wall of the stage. Once the play was over, she'd pull open the back curtain and everyone—including Marcus—would see what she'd written there.

She swung the rope a little closer to the back wall, her costume bunching up around her. If she fell, maybe it would give her some extra padding as she hit the stage.

Lena shuddered at the thought and dipped the paintbrush in the tin of red that she'd found backstage. Then she started smearing the wall with big, jagged letters. She ignored the dripping above her that must have been coming from the leaky pipe, even when a few drops of water rolled off the wooden rafters and plunked onto her forehead.

Meanwhile, the play was going on behind her, right on the other side of the curtain. Ironically, she was getting more stage time now than she would have if she'd still been a playing card.

She expected to be upset at the thought of the show happening without her, but the truth was she'd never really felt like part of the play. She hadn't let herself be part of it. As much as she'd disagreed with Mr. Jackson's methods, she'd never even tried to trust the process. And so far, the show seemed to be going well. She'd been worried for nothing.

As she painted the last letter, Lena finally relaxed a little. She'd done it! And she hadn't died! She started to hoist herself back up, but then she noticed an odd silence on the stage. The scene wasn't over, but no one was speaking. She realized that Emery's line was next. He must have forgotten it!

Her mind raced, trying to think what to do. Emery was probably only a couple feet below her, perched on a platform painted to look like an oversized tree branch. If she could lean in and whisper his line to him through the curtain, maybe he'd hear her.

Abigail repeated her line, as if trying to prompt Emery. "How do you know I'm mad?"

But there was only more silence.

"You must be or you wouldn't have come here," Lena whispered into the curtain.

"Huh?" she heard Emery say.

Lena repeated the line, louder, but it was clear Emery still couldn't hear her. She had to get closer. She grabbed on to the rope more tightly and pushed off the back wall with her legs so that she'd swing a little closer to the curtain. But she pushed off too hard, and—oh no!—started to swing *through* the curtain!

Before she could even think about jumping off—*crack!*—something above her snapped. She barely had time to scream before she burst through the curtain and hurtled toward the stage.

chapter 37

This was it. Lena was about to die. Would another soul collector guide her soul to the After? Or would she be expected to get there by herself? She didn't know whether to find that hilarious or horrible.

But the crash never came. Instead, something yanked her upward, like a giant rubber band. She opened her eyes to find herself dangling about six feet above the stage. Somehow she'd managed to grab the end of the rope, which was still magically attached to the half-broken rafter. Now that it was in pieces, she saw just how wet and spongy the wooden rafter was. It was a miracle she hadn't fallen sooner.

As her eyes focused on the stage below her, the first face she saw was Marcus's. He was standing below her, staring up with a look of shock. She couldn't help noticing that his clothes were wet and smeared with green.

"Are you okay?" he called up to her. Lena realized that there were other people around him. Lots of them. And they all looked as stunned as he did.

"Don't move!" Mr. Jackson said. "We'll get you down from there. Someone get a ladder!"

"I thought you were a piñata dropping from the ceiling," Abigail said. Abigail who was playing the lead in the play. The play that Lena had just accidentally ruined. Oops. Though, to be fair, it had already been at a pretty big standstill.

Lena glanced out at the audience and saw people staring at her with rapt expressions on their faces. At least they were enjoying the show, even if it wasn't the one they'd paid to watch.

"What were you doing up there?" Marcus called.

Lena let out a dry laugh as she tried to grip the rope more tightly, but her hands were getting tired and sweaty. "My big romantic gesture."

"Huh?" Marcus said.

"Check behind the back curtain."

Marcus looked at her like she was delirious, but when she insisted, he walked over and threw aside the edge of the curtain. Then he smiled and pulled it open the rest of the way. There, in big red letters that were a little sloppier than Lena had been hoping for, she'd written: *I'm sorry, Marcus.* And then, in small letters underneath, she'd added: *PS Look down.*

At the foot of the wall, she'd placed the two models that she'd managed to get back from Caspar.

"How did you get these?" Marcus cried, scooping up the models, his face glowing with happiness. Then he seemed to snap back to reality, and he marched back over to her. "Are you crazy? Why would you risk your life to do that?"

"Because I...because you're my soul mate," she said. Even though it was cheesy and even though Lena wasn't sure she actually believed in soul mates, that didn't matter. Because at that moment, it felt absolutely true. Mr. Watts had told her to "find her fun." But she didn't need to find it. She already had it.

"And you're mine," Marcus said without hesitation. As if he knew it with every inch of his being.

Lena felt her chest filling with warmth, but suddenly she realized her hands were cramping up. "I don't think I can hold on for much longer."

"Where is that ladder?" Mr. Jackson hollered.

"Marcus, I'm going to fall!" she cried.

"We'll catch you!" He grabbed the other kids onstage and had them join arms until they were a human net underneath her. "Okay, jump."

Lena closed her eyes. "No way. I'll die." Knowing there was an After was comforting when it came to other people's demises, but Lena wasn't ready to see the afterlife yet, not for a long while.

"Come on!" Marcus said. "It's okay. We'll catch you. I promise."

Lena opened one eye, but her entire body was pounding with panic. What if they dropped her the way she'd accidentally dropped Connie? She'd been trying to help her, but what if it all went wrong again?

"Jump!" Abigail said. "Come on!"

"Lena," Marcus said, looking her right in the eye. "You'll be fine. Trust me."

And she realized in that moment that she did trust him. Totally and completely. So she closed her eyes, took a deep breath, and let go of the rope.

When Lena was on solid ground again, Marcus threw his arms around her. It felt so good to hug her that he didn't want to let go.

Just then, someone ran onto the stage holding a ladder, and Mr. Jackson turned to the audience and said, "We'll take a short intermission and get the show going again soon." Then he shooed everyone off the stage, and Marcus heard him say to Lena, "I'll deal with you later."

"If that fall didn't kill me, I'm pretty sure Mr. Jackson will," Lena said to Marcus, but she was laughing.

He realized suddenly that Lena's stunt must have been the "ruined by red" that Natalie had foreseen. But the play hadn't been ruined, only disrupted. So the future wasn't set after all. That meant Marcus and Lena being apart didn't have to happen either.

Marcus grabbed Lena's hand and pulled her away from the stage. "I need to talk to you," he said.

"You smell different," she said as she followed him down the hallway.

"I do?" Then he realized. "Oh, I stopped wearing my dad's cologne. I know you liked it and everything, but—"

"No," she said. "It's a good different. You smell more like... well, like you."

As they went into the band room, which was empty except for a few oversized instruments in the back, Marcus tried to think of what to say. He needed to tell her that he was done trying to make their relationship perfect, and that even if it meant never using his powers again, he wanted to be with her.

Before he could say a word though, she said, "Marcus, I don't want us to be broken up. I was scared. I guess it's been hard for me to trust anybody ever since my mom left, but I want to trust you. I *do* trust you. And I swear I won't keep things from you ever again, okay?"

Marcus couldn't help himself. He grabbed her and kissed her right there in front of the tuba. The minute their lips touched, he felt a static shock race through his entire body. And there was a feeling he couldn't quite describe, something that told him that everything was right, as if the world had clicked into focus around him.

"Wow," he said when they finally broke apart. "Lena—"

But she cut him off. "Marcus, look!"

He glanced down and gasped. The air around their feet seemed to be glowing.

"That means we're back to normal, doesn't it?" Lena asked.

"But what about our emotions?" he asked. "Won't everything get messed up again because of the connection between us?"

Lena shook her head. "I don't think so, not if we're careful. Eddie said we have to be in sync with each other, that's all. I thought we were, but…"

"But we were fooling ourselves," Marcus said, remembering how convinced he'd been that their relationship was perfect. Maybe that was what that feeling during their kiss meant, that they were finally on the same frequency. And this time, he had a feeling they'd stay that way, like two radios, side by side, playing the same tune.

chapter 38

Lena took Marcus's hand, and together they stood in the wings watching the rest of the play. She had to admit that it was great. Emery stammered on a few of his lines, and a couple of entrances were off, but everyone seemed to really know their characters. And best of all, they were clearly having fun. Maybe Mr. Jackson's methods weren't so terrible after all.

When the final curtain closed and the lights came back on, the cast let out a collective cheer. Then everyone started hugging and laughing. Lena stood back and watched the merriment, happy for them and a little sad for herself. But there would be other plays. If she'd gotten into this one, she could get into those too.

"Lena! What were you thinking, nearly killing yourself on my stage?" Mr. Jackson demanded, marching over to her.

"I'm sorry," she said. "I don't know what I was thinking."

He sighed. "Okay, well don't let it happen again." Then he gave her a wink. "But you sure know how to liven up a production!" Then he bustled off to congratulate the members of the cast.

Hayleigh emerged from the crowd, and she and Abigail stared at one other for a long moment. Lena held her breath, afraid they might start trying to rip each other's hair out. Then Lena noticed something. The sparks around them seemed to be gone. Maybe the whole mess with Emery was finally over!

Instead of starting another argument, Hayleigh burst into tears and ran over to give Abigail a monstrous hug. "I'm so sorry!" she said in between sobs. "I don't know what I was thinking!"

Abigail was crying too. "It's okay. I don't know what I was thinking either. But we're okay now, aren't we?" Then she glanced at Lena. "All three of us?" Hayleigh nodded and pulled Lena into the hug too.

As her friends went off to find their families, Lena heard Marcus calling her name. "Look at Emery," he said.

Lena peered at him across the stage, expecting to see the sparks were gone around him too. But they weren't.

"Oh no," she said. "Does that mean he's still into one of my friends?" The fighting would continue after all.

Marcus grinned and pointed to Justin Alvarez.

Lena squinted. When she looked closer, she realized that the light wasn't between Emery and Abigail *or* Emery and Hayleigh. The sparks were bouncing around between Emery and Justin!

"The day I zapped them at lunch, Justin was there too, sitting next to Emery," Marcus whispered. "I think they were supposed to be the ones matched all along."

Lena shook her head in wonder, hoping that the sparks between them were strong enough to survive. Maybe this time, things would finally work out the way they were meant to.

She turned to Marcus and took his hand in hers, but then she noticed her mom standing at the foot of the stage.

"Mom, what are you doing here?"

"I couldn't miss your big acting debut, could I?" She laughed lightly. "I didn't know you were going to be the star of the show."

With everything that had happened, Lena realized she'd never told her mom that she wasn't in the play anymore. "But aren't you supposed to be in Arizona?" Lena asked. "What about your job?"

"I realized I didn't want to go back, not without you. Not even for a few weeks. And if you decide you never want to go to Arizona, then I'll find a way to move back here."

Lena could only stare for a minute. Her mom was going to give up her new life, the life she'd worked so hard for, for her?

"Now that I have you back, Lena, I'm not letting you go," her mom added. "Trust me."

For the first time in years, Lena had the urge to throw her arms around her mom and give her a giant hug. And even though she felt awkward at first, she did just that. As her mom wrapped her arms around her, Lena felt déjà vu sweep through her body. She'd forgotten—or hadn't wanted to remember—how safe and warm her mom's hugs had always been, and how right they felt. But she wasn't going to forget again.

"So that means you'll be here for Christmas?" Lena asked.

"As long as that's okay with you," her mom said.

Lena smiled. She couldn't wait to give her mom the quilt she'd made. Somehow, it felt like the perfect way to start things over between them.

"You know, Eddie could be wrong," Marcus said after Lena had seen her mom off. "We thought our powers were back to normal before, and they weren't."

"We'll figure it out. We always do." Lena felt sure of it.

Marcus nodded. "And when you go to Arizona during winter vacation, we'll figure that out too."

"What are you talking about?"

"Natalie said that in the future, you and I would be apart. I thought that meant we were going to break up, but now I think maybe it means we're going to be in different places. At least for a little while."

"But what about *A Midsummer Night's Dream*? You went to

so much trouble for those tickets!" She gave him a little nudge with her elbow. "If you still want to go with me, that is."

"Of course I do," he said. "But we can switch the tickets for another date. You need to go be with your mom."

"What about my dad? I can't leave him here alone," Lena started to protest, but she knew that wasn't an excuse. Her dad had Viv now. If Lena left, he'd miss her, but he'd be fine. "I...I don't know if I can survive without you there," she finally admitted. "What if it's too awkward, or what if I hate it there, or what if..." She sighed. "What if I love it and I want to stay? What will we do then?"

Marcus smiled and squeezed her hand. "It won't be perfect, but we'll make it work. We always do."

epilogue

E ddie stood in the shadows of the nearly empty auditorium.
"Yes, ma'am," he said into his phone. "The chain reaction has finally stopped. Since the assignment was successful, I was hoping my daughter could stay on as my assistant."

He glanced at Natalie, who was slumped in a nearby seat. Eddie had never thought he could feel responsible for another person like he had since she'd come into his life, although in truth, he'd already had a little practice. Over the past few months, he'd found himself thinking of Lena and Marcus as his own special assignments.

"Thank you, ma'am. Natalie will be glad to hear it." He listened for a long time, nodding. "I know Lena and Marcus have caused more trouble than you expected, but everything should be back to normal now, shouldn't it?"

As he listened, his face tightened. He glanced at Lena and Marcus, who were walking, hand in hand, across the stage. They looked so happy. He hated the thought of them having to face anything else, but if what the boss lady said was true, then the future was as uncertain as ever.

"I understand, ma'am," Eddie said finally. "I'll do what I can to prepare them, but the rest will be up to them."

# acknowledgments

It turns out writing a novel with a newborn baby in the house is hard! My thanks to Babcia Kamila and Grandma Mary for watching the wee one while I hid away with my laptop. Eternal thanks to Ammi-Joan Paquette and Aubrey Poole for spot-on feedback and guidance, and to my family and friends for always cheering me on. Thank you to Heather Kelly for helping me with pesky world-building stuff and to Ray Brierly for lending me his brain when mine wasn't working.

 about the author →

Anna Staniszewski was a Writer-in-Residence at the Boston Public Library and a winner of the PEN New England Discovery Award. She lives outside Boston with her family and teaches at Simmons College. When she's not writing, Anna reads as much as she can, takes the dog for long walks, and tries to keep her magical powers under wraps. Visit her at www.annastan.com.

THE DIRT DIARY SERIES

Anna Staniszewski

The Dirt Diary

EIGHTH GRADE NEVER SMELLED SO BAD.

Rachel Lee didn't think anything could be worse than her parents splitting up. She was wrong. Working for her mom's new house-cleaning business puts Rachel in the dirty bathrooms of the most popular kids in the eighth grade. Which does not help her already loser-ish reputation. But her new job has surprising perks: enough dirt on the in-crowd to fill up her (until recently) boring diary. She never intended to reveal her secrets, but when the hottest guy in school pays her to spy on his girlfriend, Rachel decides to get her hands dirty.

The Prank List

Anna Staniszewski

TO SAVE HER MOM'S CLEANING BUSINESS, RACHEL'S ABOUT TO GET HER HANDS DIRTY—AGAIN.

Rachel Lee is having the best summer ever taking a baking class and flirting with her almost-sort-of-boyfriend Evan—until a rival cleaning business swoops into town, stealing her mom's clients. Rachel never thought she'd fight for the right to clean toilets, but she has to save her mom's business. Nothing can distract her from her mission...except maybe Whit, the cute new guy in cooking class. Then she discovers something about Whit that could change everything. After destroying her Dirt Diary, Rachel thought she was done with secrets, but to save her family's business, Rachel's going to have to get her hands dirty. Again.

The Gossip File

Anna Staniszewski

SOME THINGS ARE BEST KEPT SECRET...

Rachel is spending the holiday break with her dad and soon-to-be step-monster, Ellie. Thank goodness her BFF Marisol gets to come with. But when Rachel meets a new group of kids and realizes she can leave her loser status back home, quirky Marisol gets left behind. Bored and abandoned, Marisol starts a Gossip File, collecting info on the locals. When the gossip includes some dirt on Ellie, Rachel has to decide if getting the truth is worth risking her new cool-girl persona...

THE
MY VERY UNFAIRY
TALE LIFE SERIES
Anna Staniszewski

My Very UnFairy Tale Life

THIS IS ONE DAMSEL THAT DOESN'T NEED RESCUING.

Jenny has spent the last two years as an adventurer helping magical kingdoms around the universe. But it's a thankless job, leaving her no time for school or friends. She'd almost rather take a math test than rescue yet another magical creature! When Jenny is sent on yet another mission, she has a tough choice to make: quit and have her normal life back, or fulfill her promise and go into a battle she doesn't think she can win.

My Epic Fairy Tale Fail

FAIRY TALES DO COME TRUE. UNFORTUNATELY.

Jenny has finally accepted her life of magic and mayhem as savior of fairy tale kingdoms, but that doesn't mean the job's any easier. Her new mission is to travel to the Land of Tales to defeat an evil witch and complete three Impossible Tasks. Throw in some school friends, a bumbling knight, a rhyming troll, and a giant bird, and happily ever after starts looking far, far away. But with her parents' fate on the line, this is one happy ending Jenny is determined to deliver.

My Sort of Fairy Tale Ending

HAPPILY EVER AFTER? YEAH, RIGHT.

Jenny's search for her parents leads her to Fairyland, a rundown amusement park filled with creepily happy fairies and disgruntled leprechauns. Despite the fairies' kindness, she knows they are keeping her parents from her. If only they would stop being so happy all the time—it's starting to weird her out! With the help of a fairy-boy and some rebellious leprechauns, Jenny finds a way to rescue her parents, but at the expense of putting all magical worlds in danger. Now Jenny must decide how far she is willing to go to put her family back together.